D0173531

I suddenly realized what situation I was in. I was walking up the street beside *Maxine*. There was no *way* I wanted to be there. I tried to think of an excuse.

"I'm in a hurry," I said. "I got to get back and do my homework."

"I'm in a hurry, too," she says. "I left Ronald home by himself, sitting by the TV. I put on *Lassie*. He likes that."

I felt pretty awkward when she said that. What if Bobby and Chris and all them were down there messing around, like they did, sometimes. They wouldn't know she wasn't in there, too. They wouldn't pick on Ronald if they knew. I wondered if she recognized me from those times on the street.

Also by Jane Leslie Conly

Racso and the Rats of NIMH

R-T, Margaret, and the Rats of NIMH

Crazy Lady!

by Jane Leslie Conly

A LAURA GERINGER BOOK

HarperTrophy
A Division of HarperCollinsPublishers

Crazy Lady!

Copyright © 1993 by Jane Leslie Conly

All rights reserved. No part of this book may be used or reproduced in any manner whatsoever without written permission except in the case of brief quotations embodied in critical articles and reviews. Printed in the United States of America. For information address HarperCollins Children's Books, a division of HarperCollins Publishers, 10 East 53rd Street, New York, NY 10022.

Library of Congress Cataloging-in-Publication Data

Conly, Jane Leslie

Crazy lady! / by Jane Leslie Conly.

   p.   cm.

"A Laura Geringer book."

Summary: As he tries to come to terms with his mother's death, Vernon finds solace in his growing relationship with the neighborhood outcasts, an alcoholic and her retarded son.

   ISBN 0-06-021357-4. — ISBN 0-06-021360-4 (lib. bdg.)

   ISBN 0-06-440517-0 (pbk.)

   [1. Interpersonal relationships—Fiction.   2. Prejudices—Fiction.   3. Death—Fiction.   4. Alcoholics—Fiction.   5. Mentally handicapped—Fiction.]

PZ7.C761846Cr   1993   92-18348

[Fic]—dc20   CIP

                                                             AC

Typography by Joyce Hopkins

❖

First Harper Trophy edition, 1995.

For Pete

Crazy Lady!

1

"SOMETIMES I still dream about them, even though it's been two years since it happened," I told Miss Annie. "I dream she's walking down the street, right in the middle like she always did, with Ronald on her arm. She's wearing dark glasses and a funny hat and purple pants, and she sways back and forth when she walks. Ronald looks like himself—tall and thin. He's all pop-eyed, like he's scared someone's going to hurt him. And his mouth opens like he wants to talk, but he can't."

"I remember that look." Miss Annie nodded.

"Then the kids come, and she starts shouting, and they do, too: 'Crazy Lady!' And she'll cuss them and hold on to Ronald, and they laugh and cuss right back." I stopped. "I must have had that dream a hundred times," I confessed.

Miss Annie nodded again, a quick little nod. She looks like she'll break if she moves more than just a bit. Lately her dark skin is stretched tight across her bones, as if it shrank in the wash and didn't stretch out again. But her mind is sharp.

"Vernon," she said, "you ought to tell that story to someone. Or else write it down. Not just the dream— the whole thing."

I laughed. "You know me better than that. I'm not going to spend the summer writing something I don't have to. School is bad enough."

She looked out the window for a moment, as if the answer was there. "That's what those dreams want. They want to be told."

"A dream can't want something, Miss Annie."

"It can, too." She smiled. "Dreams can make you so scared or addled or miserable that you'll do whatever you have to just to be free of them."

"Not me." I shook my head like I had everything under control. "I just tell them to go away and leave me alone."

"You might as well stick a seed in the ground and tell it not to grow," Miss Annie said. "It will come out of the dark one way or another."

"It won't either," I said.

But, of course, it did.

As for me, I grew up with a million kids. There are five just in my family: Steph, Tony, me, Sandra, and

Ben. Steph lives out in the suburbs now; she's married, and she works in a lab. And Tony is in college. He's the first one in our family to go. He graduated from Tech last year and got a scholarship.

My family's Catholic. When we were little, we used to walk to church in a long line, holding hands. Somebody took a picture of that, and I love to look at it. It's like we're the whole world, we look so different: some blond, some dark, some with long hair, some real short, Tony already tall, and Ben sitting like a little puppet on Daddy's arm. My mom's in the picture, too. I've studied her face. Sometimes I put my finger on it like I could really touch her. The way she looks in that picture is just the way she was: kind and honest and brave. She had dark eyes and hair and she was heavy, so she usually wore pants and a baggy shirt, even to church. People say I look like her, but I'm not sure. I'm big for my age, and my eyes are brown, and my hair is dark brown, which is the way she was.

My mom died of a stroke three years ago. She was at her job, sitting at a sewing machine in a factory over in Hampden, and she keeled over. We kids didn't know anything about it. We came home from school and we played just like always, and ate up half the food in the refrigerator, which we weren't supposed to do. And she didn't come home, and we kept on waiting, and finally Steph said, "We ought to do our homework." So some of them—not me—were doing it, and Daddy came in. We knew something bad had happened then. He worked

3

the three-to-eleven shift, so he'd come home right in the middle of work. And his eyes were red. I'd never seen him cry before; I'd never even thought that he *could* cry. And he told us.

We've gotten along without her, but it's been hard. My dad is a quiet person. He's frail-looking, and after Mom died he seemed to get paler and smaller. Sometimes we didn't even notice he was home, with all the noise us kids made. It didn't use to be like that. I remember times when he'd come in from work and put one finger to his lips to keep us quiet. He'd line us up behind him. We'd creep into the kitchen and grab Mom from behind. She'd shriek and swat at us, and we'd fall down laughing.

It's not his fault things changed. Daddy will do anything for you. He never yells, and if he sees something is bothering you, he'll try to make you feel better. He'll buy you a candy bar and slip it to you behind his back so the other kids don't see. He'll give you a dollar, or tell you something he overheard about the Orioles' latest trade, or he'll sit down and try to work your problem out one point at a time. He tries, but he can't be Mom.

You see, Mom could make you feel special even if you had a face like a garbage-can lid. She hugged you on the outside and the inside, too. I'm the one in the family who was bad in school. I tried, but when the report cards came out, it was always the same: mine was the worst. I failed third grade and barely slid by the next year. Mom never blamed me. She said, "Some

4

kids, like Tony, find it easy to learn, and that's good. But the ones I admire most are the ones who keep on trying, even when it's hard. The ones who hang in there even when they don't end up on top. Those children are very special."

Special. I blushed when she said that, and I told myself she could see what the teachers couldn't: deep down inside I *was* smart. But that was a secret between us. When she died, the secret died, too—not all at once, but slowly, fading like the picture on a worn T-shirt until finally even the outlines disappeared. Then I started to see myself like everyone else did: a big clunky kid, trying to slip by without being noticed, trying to pass.

2

I WANT YOU TO KNOW ABOUT our neighborhood. It's called Tenley Heights. Why anybody named it that is beyond me. There's only one hill in the whole place, and it's not that big. In fact, the whole neighborhood is only five blocks long and three blocks wide. It's squeezed into the upper center of the city, with a highway on each side of it and the baseball stadium on the north end. It's where the Orioles play—you know, the American League team.

There's a lot of people who've lived in Tenley Heights their whole life—me, for example. I was born at City Hospital a mile away. Then Mom brought me back to the brick rowhouse where we live right now. We know every single family on both sides of the block, mostly because of the kids. The houses are narrow and dark, so when it's daylight nobody stays inside. They come out on the porches, and then the kids start crossing over, this one to that house and that one over here; a gang on the corner and another crowd hanging in front of Milt's store. It's not like in the suburbs, where you have to be careful about being kidnapped. Any kidnapper could tell right away that people in Tenley Heights don't have money for ransom.

It's rough around here, too. You wouldn't think so most of the time, when kids are playing together and mothers are talking up and down the porch rows; but there've been some murders. Milt's brother Joe got killed when the store was robbed, and a gang of boys killed a black guy in the stadium parking lot three years ago. For a long time Daddy didn't like it when the blacks started moving in, but after the Murphys moved next door he changed his mind. Chris Murphy is a real good friend of mine. He and I used to say we were going to be the greatest shortstop–second-base combination that ever lived. We had plans to get signed on the Orioles when we were both eighteen, play for a couple of years, and become millionaires.

But that's beside the point, because what I really need to tell you is about the next block down. To put it bluntly, it's a slum. Most of the houses there are wood, and some of them look stuck together, like a little kid built them out of leftover boards and shingles. People live down there with their windows broken out all year round. Some of the walls have been patched so many times, they look like quilts, and then there'll be a hole anyway, so you can see right through. I didn't go down there much until I met Maxine and Ronald and their friend Miss Annie. That was 1981, the year I started junior high.

That's when it dawned on me I was never going to be a baseball star. Before then I'd spent about a hundred hours a week throwing a tennis ball against a little square that we'd painted onto the back wall of someone's garage. Sometimes Chris would bat, and if Bobby came along one of us would do the fielding. I was sure I was pretty good; the big question in my mind was: pitcher or shortstop? I'd go to bed at night thinking it over. Sometimes I'd lie there and make the decision once and for all. Then I'd turn over and tell Tony, "Guess what? I've got it all thought out."

"Yeah, Vernon," he'd sigh. "What is it?"

"Pitcher. Because in the World Series that's what matters in the long run: the pitching. Look at Sandy Koufax. Anybody on the street knows the name Sandy Koufax. You can say Ozzie Smith or Mark Bellanger till you're blue in the face and they won't know it, but they'll know Sandy Koufax."

"Vernon, I'm glad for you," Tony would say. "I'm glad you finally figured it out."

"Yeah." But as soon as I'd said that, I'd begin to have my doubts all over again. Pitchers could wear out in a year or two, but a good infielder could last a long time. And Chris and I were a pretty good combination. We could turn our end of a double play real good. I'd jerk my arm, like I was tossing the ball to Chris, and Tony would get mad.

"Can't you lay still? I got to get some rest. I got a science test tomorrow."

"Big deal," I'd say. "Maybe you'll get a B for once. Wouldn't that break your heart?"

"Shut up, dimwit."

"Shut up yourself." Tony lorded it over me because of his grades, but I was stronger than him, and he knew it. I jerked my arm again, deliberately. He didn't say anything. Pitcher or shortstop? I asked myself. I fell asleep with my mind still not made up.

That fall Chris and I tried out for the school team, and we never came close. If I'd spent a hundred hours a week throwing that ball, there must have been kids who spent a thousand, they were so much better than me. At first I couldn't believe it. But it was true. In our neighborhood I was one of the best, but at junior high I was nothing.

It was a rough year. Like I said, I'd been held back once, so I was a year older and a lot bigger than most of the other kids. And Mom had died the year before. I didn't have anyone to talk to about how lonely I felt. I'd have to get my breakfast, get dressed, and catch the bus on time. Lots of times Daddy worked a double shift, so we didn't see him in the morning at all. Steph would look after the little guys, but I was too big for that. I'd get to school and notice that my socks didn't match, or that a button had fallen off my shirt, and all day I'd feel bad. I'd hunker down in the last seat and hope the teachers wouldn't call on me, and usually they didn't. But when I went home and spread the homework on the kitchen table, it might as well have been Chinese.

I guess I needed something fun to do, and I tried to find it. The kids at school came from all over the place. They were nice. We'd have a good time at lunch, and now and then we'd get something going in homeroom or in the halls between classes. But at three o'clock we'd get on the buses and go back to our own neighborhoods.

And in the neighborhood something funny had happened, without me realizing it. I found out that once you're in junior high, you're too big for lots of the stuff you used to do before. Like the programs they have at the library or up at the rec are all for elementary kids. There's not much point in spending your life tossing a baseball once you find out you aren't going to make it big. At the same time you're too young for an after-school job—you have to be fifteen to get a work permit. So a whole group of us was stuck with nothing to do.

3

BOBBY SULLIVAN STARTED IT. We were hanging around on the corner, watching the cars go by and talking about what kind we wanted. Bobby asked did any of us know how to drive, and a couple of us—me and Chris and Jerry Roland—said yes. Bobby said, "I know how to hot wire a Toyota."

Chris said, "Bobby, you talk so big."

"I do," says Bobby. "If we can find one that ain't locked up, I'll show you."

"Wait a minute," Chris said. "I'm not going to be party to stealing a car. I got other things to do."

"I'm not going to steal it—I'm not even going to break into it. Didn't you hear what I said? I said if I can find one that's already open, I'll show you."

"I don't know, Bobby." I was curious about whether he could do it, and whether he would do it, but I didn't want to get into trouble either.

"Look. All you guys got to do is help me find it. Then you can walk up the street and stand on the corner if you want to. You just listen and you'll hear me start it up, and then I'll get out."

It didn't seem like it would do any harm, so we said okay, and we looked around the neighborhood to see if we could find one that wasn't locked. But we couldn't find any. We did find a couple of unlocked cars, a Chevrolet and a Buick, but Bobby had never claimed he could hot wire those. Nevertheless he did get in and try, and we stood up on the corner and watched. But after a while he got out—no luck.

We tried to think of something else to do. It was like we wanted to make up for the excitement we'd lost by Bobby not being able to start those cars.

"We could go up to Woolworth's and snitch some candy bars," somebody said. Most of the kids did it. We had a friend, Michael, who worked up there. He was a couple of years older than us, and he knew we did it, but he never said anything. He used to do it himself.

"Okay." Everybody thought that was all right, not anything exciting but it would pass the time. So we went up there and Chris was the cover, because he had two dollars and because his old man would kill him if he got caught stealing. So we milled around and caused a little confusion and by the time we got out I had a couple of Hershey bars jammed in my pocket. I ate them fast, to destroy the evidence. We wandered back down onto my block. It was about a half hour till suppertime.

That was when we saw them. I mean really *saw*. They'd been around for years, but I hadn't paid much attention.

"Look at that," Bobby said.

We looked.

A woman was coming up the middle of the street. She was short and stocky, and her hair stuck out to the sides. She was wearing dark glasses and smoking a cigarette, and on the top of her head was a big red hat with a tassel on it. She was moving as if she didn't want anyone to get in her way.

The kid who was holding on to her was even stranger than she was. He was tall and skinny—real skinny. His skin was broken out, which made me think he was a teenager, but you couldn't be sure. The look on his face was more like a little kid's: scared. His eyes were open wide, and his mouth was working as if he wanted to talk, and he was holding tight to her arm.

"She's something else," Jerry said. "What's her name?"

"Maxine Flooter. The little kids call her the crazy lady. And that's her goofy son, Ronald."

Maxine must have guessed we were talking about her. "Hey, you boys," she yelled. "You stay out of my way."

"Nobody's getting in your way," Bobby said.

"You stay out of my way," she repeated. "This is the

13

United States of America. I can walk down the street if I want to."

"I ain't in your way," Bobby said. Then he did something mean. He threw a candy-bar wrapper out in front of them. "There's some candy for your baby," he said.

She bent over and picked it up, and when she saw it was empty, she let out a string of cussing like I never heard in my life. I couldn't believe it. It was like getting a whole new education.

We laughed it up. Then Jerry threw a couple of pinecones at her. They hit her coat. She screeched like a tomcat.

"I'll knock you halfway to Alabama!" she shouted. She swung her pocketbook over her head.

Jerry laughed, but I could tell he was nervous.

"Go ahead—throw it!" he yelled.

"I wish I could. I'd send you flying up the street like a Ping-Pong ball."

"What's stopping you?"

"Your dirty face."

"I took a bath last night. That's more than you or your son."

She dropped the pocketbook and glared. "Ronald's *clean*. I wash him every day with Ivory soap. There's not a day Ronald goes to school dirty."

We stared at Ronald. He was clinging to Maxine like a baby. "You've got him all shook up," she said. "Shame on you."

"You started it!"

"I did not! We were walking down the street minding our own business!" She crossed her arms over her chest and stuck her face out. "You boys were looking for trouble."

Bobby cussed. "You *are* crazy."

"You better not bother Ronald!" she hollered. "You better leave him alone!"

Just then Frank Gilberti came out of his house. He's a retired Italian guy who lives across the street from us.

"These boys are picking on me!" Maxine yelled. "They're picking on Ronald, too!"

"Go on by," he said quietly. He stood there while she went down the street.

"We didn't do nothing," Bobby called. Since she was gone he went on home, and Jerry did, too.

"Good night, Vernon," Mr. Frank said as I opened my door. "Tell your papa I said hey."

I nodded and went inside.

After that we made a habit of standing on the corner to see if she'd come by with Ronald. Somebody found out that he went to a school for retarded kids, and that a special bus brought him home every day around three thirty. Maxine was always there to get him off the bus. Sometimes they went into their house and didn't come out again. But other days she'd head right up the center of the street toward the shopping strip along the highway. She wouldn't move for anyone; bikes and cars had to go around her.

Her house was something else, just like she was. It was in the block I told you about, and it was probably the worst house there. It was a duplex; the house that hooked onto it was painted green and had a window box with flowers out front. I pitied whoever that was, living next door to Maxine. Her yard was muddy, with a lot of broken-up boards lying in it. The porch had a hole in the floor big enough for a cow to fall through. And instead of curtains she had blankets hung over the windows so you couldn't see inside. You could hear, though; if you went up to the door, there would be an explosion of barks like little gunshots. Then you'd hear her scream, "BROWNIE! Be quiet, Brownie!" So we figured that was her dog.

We wanted to know all about her, 'cause there wasn't anyone else like her in the neighborhood. There were lots of people who kept to themselves, and there were weirdos, too. Like Brenda Danger, who weighed about three hundred pounds and shaved her head, and Andy, who walked around with three or four cameras around his neck but never took a picture. There were winos and pushers and people who got into fights on Saturday night. But there wasn't anybody else who walked right down the middle of the street and shouted at you if you looked her way.

The little things we did, I guess we thought she deserved them. Like if we snitched candy, we'd always throw the wrappers in her yard. Sometimes we'd draw pictures of her on notebook paper and leave them up on the porch. Bobby would write stuff like "You must be named Marilyn Monroe" or "I love you" on the papers. A couple of times we put fake money up against her door, hoping she'd think it was real. And another time Bobby took off his underwear and left it hanging on her doorknob.

But what we liked most was to agitate her so she'd put on a show. If she was in the house and you knocked on the door, she knew better than to open it. So we had to wait until she came out. Sometimes we'd stand up on the corner and wait, but other times we'd crouch with our backs to the hedge outside her house. When we'd hear the door open, we'd sit tight, just glancing over our shoulders. Just as she and Ronald were coming out on the sidewalk, we'd jump up and shout, "Hey, Maxine!" Sometimes Bobby would say, "Hi, your majesty." But it didn't really matter what it was: anything we said would make her pop her cork.

It was a wonder she had any voice left, the way she carried on. She'd scream at us and cuss us and tell us what she thought. She'd say she was going to ship us over to the Ayatollah and have him burn our hides alive. She'd say she knew a doctor who was developing a mind poison you could shoot with darts, and we were going to be his first targets. She'd say she was a friend of the bionic man, and he'd told her he was going to come over here and tear us apart the day after tomorrow.

"I'm *terrified*," somebody would say.

17

"You better be," she'd answer. "An angel told me that you're going to die in your sleep tonight."

"I'm scared," I'd say. "I'm really scared."

Every now and then a grown-up would scold us about the way we carried on with Maxine: "Why don't you leave her alone? You all cause such a racket I can't hear my TV show." Or they'd say, "You're going to make Milt rich selling liquor, the way you get her so riled up. She's a drunk, you know."

Her son Ronald was always scared. He'd look at us and then he'd look at Maxine and he'd look like he wanted to disappear. A few times I caught myself feeling sorry for him. Then I got my report card, and I stopped thinking about Ronald or Maxine.

4

I'LL PUT THE BEST FIRST: C in shop; C in gym; D in math; D in earth science; F in English; and F in French. Why I thought I could do French when I can't hardly speak my own language is more than I can say. Anyway, I could see that if things didn't get better, I was going to be in seventh grade again next year. The thought was awful. Here I was, big for my age and already spending most of the day trying to sink down in my seat and disappear. If things got worse next year, I wasn't sure I could take it. I talked to Daddy, but he didn't know what to say. He quit school when he was in fourth grade because he couldn't read. He's missed promotions because of that.

The thought of going through seventh grade again was driving me crazy. I asked Steph what I could do. She thought about it and said the guidance counselor at school might have some ideas, and I should make an appointment with her. She felt bad she couldn't tutor me. She was working on some kind of experiment with the Science Club. If it came out right, she said, she'd get a good job when she graduated.

I even asked Chris if he had any ideas. His grades were good: mostly B's and C's. One day he said he'd try to help me. He came over and we sat down at the kitchen table. He showed me how to do problems with percents. I asked him so many questions that by the time he was done explaining, he couldn't remember how to do the problems himself. "You're thinking too deep about it," he said, sipping his glass of Coke. "You got to do exactly what they say and don't ask questions." But that didn't work for me.

I went to the guidance counselor during gym period. She was a nice lady with a little office just to one side of the library. Her name was Mrs. Robinson.

"Vernon," she said, "I think the answer is to get some tutoring. We have it here, after school, or you can get it at the public library, if you live near certain branches."

"I live in Tenley Heights," I murmured. I was holding my breath.

She looked on a diagram. "They don't have it over there," she said. "They have it at Upton. You know where that is?"

"Yes, ma'am." I nodded. Upton is a real rough neighborhood. There's no way I was going over there.

"If you get it here, there's a slight charge," Mrs.

20

Robinson said. "It's two dollars an hour. Do you think you can afford that?"

What was I supposed to say? We couldn't afford anything—we almost couldn't afford to eat. But I wasn't going to tell her that.

"You go home and ask your father," she said. "If he says yes, come back and I'll sign you up. And if he says no, we'll try to figure something else out. Maybe Upton."

"Thanks, Mrs. Robinson." It didn't seem polite to tell her that she hadn't been any help.

I was getting desperate. I'd go home after school and sit down at the kitchen table with my homework in front of me, and I'd try to do it. I'd try what Chris said: just do what they showed you that day, and don't ask questions. But I couldn't get the answers, because I usually didn't know how to do something else they'd taught a couple of months ago, which you had to do first before you could work the rest of the problem. Still, my teachers knew I was trying. My science teacher called me to his desk between class periods and said he'd pass me with a C if I just kept doing the work the best I could. And my shop teacher, Mr. Cole, showed me some stuff about angles using a miter box. I used that for extra homework for math. I knew French was a total loss, but I could fail one without being held back. That left English.

And then something happened you would never believe, not on your life.

5

I DIDN'T HAVE MUCH TO DO with the gang after I got in such a fix with my grades. I would hear little things now and then. I knew they'd found an unlocked Toyota, and Bobby had managed to get it started. He'd driven it partway up the block and left it parked, just for a joke. They'd gotten some pens and notebooks up at Woolworth's without being caught, but Michael had told them to lay low. Candy was one thing, I guess, and notebooks were another. They'd been messing with Maxine, too. Either Bob or Jerry had thrown a rock through her front window. She was so mad, she'd chased them up the street in her underwear. "I'll have to pay for that!" she screamed. "And it could have hit Ronald!" The thought of her chasing them like that caused me to bust a gut laughing.

One afternoon when I got home I found a note from Steph on the table. It said, "Vernon, please go up to Milt's and get five pounds of potatoes for supper. It will cost $1.09—I bought a bag on Monday, so I know." There were two dollars on top of it. I was kind of pleased, because for a long time somebody used to go with me to Milt's because he had a habit of shortchanging kids, and I wasn't much good at figuring out when that happened. So I jammed the money in my pocket and took off up there, figuring I'd try to do my homework when I got back. Like always, there was a line in the store. It was the same line whether you wanted liquor or groceries or a lottery ticket. I just kind of closed my eyes and listened to the TV play and waited for them to get to me.

It was a few minutes before I zeroed in on what was happening. There was an argument going on between Milt and the woman a few up. She kept saying, "I gave you a five."

He said something in a low voice.

"No, it's not," she said. "It's one-oh-nine. You should have given me three dollars and ninety-one cents."

I couldn't hear what he said. The man in front of me sighed.

The woman said something else, but this time it was soft. Then I heard Milt start yelling. "Five pounds of potatoes in my store will run you one forty-nine," he shouted. "It changed last month. If you want them cheaper, walk up the hill to the A&P."

She asked for her money back.

"You can't have it back," he shouted. "I'll put it on your bill. You got a bill here as long as history."

"I'm here for potatoes, too," I said. "My sister said they were a dollar nine on Monday."

"Who's that?" Milt yelled. He looked around through the plate-glass cage he sat in, and he saw me. "Another genius come to mess up my day," he said loud. "You go on up to the A&P too."

I felt my scalp getting hot, like it does when I'm mad.

"You go to hell, Milt," I hollered. "You been a cheat and a liar since you were born. And my daddy doesn't have a bill up here, so you can't say nothing about that."

"Get out of here," Milt yelled. "Just get the hell out before I call the cops."

"Call the damn cops," I said. "Go ahead." I headed for the door, but on my way out I kicked the lower rack where he kept potato chips. They went flying every which way.

"I'm going to call 'em!" he screamed. "I'm going to!"

By that time I was out. He wasn't going to call the cops. He knew, and I knew, in Tenley Heights they don't come out because somebody kicked a couple of bags of chips on the floor.

I turned the corner hard, because I was mad. And I practically ran right into her.

"Hey, you," she said. "You done good."

The voice was the voice of the woman in the store, who'd had the argument before me. But the face, and

24

all that went with it, was Maxine.

I was stuck in my tracks. I stared right at her. She looked pretty much like usual: she was wearing shades and a purple hat with a veil on it, and a shabby wool jacket. She had a big plastic pocketbook hanging on her arm.

"Thanks," I said. It was all I could manage.

"You going up the A&P to get yours?"

"I guess I'll have to," I said. "I don't have no choice."

"It's a shame, what that man gets away with. And a lot of folks is just stuck with it. I can't argue with him—I might need the credit. Once my check runs out, there's no place left to go."

"I guess."

I suddenly realized what situation I was in. I was walking up the street beside *Maxine*. There was no *way* I wanted to be there. I tried to think of an excuse.

"I'm in a hurry," I said. "I got to get back and do my homework."

"I'm in a hurry, too," she says. "I left Ronald home by himself, sitting by the TV. I put on *Lassie*. He likes that."

I felt pretty awkward when she said that. What if Bobby and Chris and all them were down there messing around, like they did sometimes. They wouldn't know she wasn't in there, too. They wouldn't pick on Ronald if they knew. I wondered if she recognized me from those times on the street.

"You give me the money and go on home," I said.

"No sense both of us walking up the hill. I'll get the potatoes and bring 'em back to your house."

"That's right nice of you," she said. And she gave me a dollar and some change.

I hotfooted it up that hill, got in the express line, and was out of there in ten minutes. I had a bag of potatoes under each arm. The whole time I was moving, my mind was working, asking: how can she be the same woman who carries on so crazy?

I got back to her house quick. Luckily the kids weren't there. I jumped over the hole in the porch and banged on the door. She opened it right away.

"I do thank you," she said.

"That's okay," I said. I couldn't wait to get away from there.

"You know what?" She was looking at me hard. Her glasses were off, so you could see her eyes. They were blue, with lines all around them.

"What?"

"I believe I knew your mama. Are you a Dibbs?"

I nodded.

"I thought so—you favor her more than the others. She was a real nice woman. It hit me hard when I heard she was dead. One winter—it must have been three or four years ago—she sewed a coat for Ronald. She got a remnant of wool at the factory and did it on her lunch hour. She must have seen us on the street, and she knew he didn't have anything decent to wear. She brought it down here and didn't expect a dime."

26

I couldn't say anything. I get a funny feeling in my throat when somebody talks about my mom.

"How y'all getting on without her?" Maxine asked. "It must be hard."

"It is," I said. I was kind of choked up.

"If there's ever anything I can do, you let me know," she said. She was getting ready to close the door.

Later I wasn't sure why I said it. It just popped out of me. "I'm failing school," I said. "If I don't find someone to help me pass English, I'll have to stay back again."

She looked kind of surprised, and thoughtful. "I might know a lady," she said, after a minute. "I'll ask her. And if she can do it, I'll come 'round your house and let you know."

6

LATER I THOUGHT, I must be the one that's crazy, telling her that. I didn't mention what happened to anyone, except to tell Steph about the price change at Milt's. "Better stay out of there for a few days," I told her. "I got heated up and lost my temper."

"I hope you told him off," Steph said. "That jerk."

Maxine didn't come up to the house, and I was glad. I didn't want everybody laughing at *me*. But a couple days later I found a note in the mailbox, just scrawled on a piece of notebook paper:

Pibbs boy, I know a lady who used to be a teacher. Come down and I'll introduss you.

Maxine

I went on down there. When I knocked on the door, she answered it right away.

"Come right in," she said. "I'll get Ronald, and we'll go on over. I asked her, and she says she'll do it."

I stood there waiting. The house was a mess. There was a big pile of clothes on the dining-room table, and others were hanging from a line strung across the room. The sofa was covered with a blanket, with an old TV beside it. There were a couple of chairs, and a calendar up on the wall. A ratty little dog was lying in one corner. He looked at me and growled.

"Shut up, Brownie. Ronald, stand up. We're going to Miss Annie's. You want to see Miss Annie?"

Ronald's head gave a quick jerk. I was surprised. I didn't know Ronald understood things.

"Put your coat on," Maxine said. "Then we'll go."

Ronald looked at me. I could tell he was afraid.

"He ain't going to bother you," Maxine said. "Come on now."

I watched while he struggled with his coat. He reminded me of a puppet—it was like someone else was controlling his arms. His mouth moved back and forth, and he glanced at me a couple of times. After a minute, he did it.

"Good for you," Maxine said. She looked at me. "He's been working on that in school."

We walked around the house and up to the other side of the duplex—the green side. Maxine knocked on the door. An old woman opened it. I groaned inside. I knew her; she used to go up and down the street every afternoon, walking with a metal cane. She always had this great big dumb grin on her face, no matter what kind of day it was. We kids called her the Lady from La-La Land, and sometimes we'd ask if she'd beam us to her planet, because it must be pretty nice, wherever it was. She never answered except to say, "Hello, boys," as if we'd said something pleasant. I hoped she didn't remember, but I had a feeling from the sharp look she gave me that she did. She was polite, though. "Come on in," she said. "Come in, all of you."

We went past her. I saw that she was using a walker now. I guess that was why she hadn't been on the street lately.

Her living room was as neat as a pin. The sofa and chairs had lace across the tops. There was a little table with a glass jar filled with candy beside the sofa. Ronald saw that right away. He kept staring at it.

"Would you like a piece of candy, Ronald?" Miss Annie asked. You would have thought from her tone that she was offering it to the president.

He nodded.

"Here you are." She took the wrapping off. He stuck the candy in his mouth.

"Sit down," Miss Annie said. We did. She was dressed in a skirt and sweater that matched. Her hair was braided and pinned up with a barrette.

"I'm not sure I know your name."

I swallowed. "Vernon Dibbs."

"Exactly what kind of problem are you having with English?"

I had to think about the answer. "I can't hardly read and I can't spell," I said. "With reading and spelling, I just can't seem to remember things, no matter if I've done them before or not. I can read a word a hundred times and I might not remember it the next time."

She looked at me with interest. "Do you know phonics? I mean, can you sound words out by the way they're spelled?"

"Sometimes I can. But sometimes they're spelled so different . . ." I shrugged. "Like you would think 'could' would be spelled c-o-o-d, but it's not."

She nodded. "Some people have problems memorizing." She paused, sizing me up. "I taught elementary school for forty years," she said. "I've had all kinds of students. I can't say for sure that I can help, but I'm willing to try."

"Oh." I could feel the smile spreading across my face. Somehow I had the feeling she *could* help me. "Thank you."

"Bring your books and your homework assignment down here each day at four o'clock," she said crisply. "We'll try for a month, and see if there's any improvement."

Miss Annie worked me like a dog. She'd seemed spacey on the sidewalk, but when it came to teaching, she was all business.

"This one now," she said, pointing to a worksheet she'd made up.

"Poor, pore, pour," I read. "The poor boy tried to pour some milk, but his face itched because some dirt was stuck in a pore."

"Very good, Vernon."

I smiled. I wasn't used to compliments on my schoolwork.

When the lesson ended, Miss Annie told me more about herself. She was still in touch with a lot of the kids she'd taught; they called and wrote to her, and sent pictures of their children. She and her husband had been one of the first black families to move to Tenley Heights. She'd lived by herself since he'd died eight years ago. Their children lived way out in California.

"They asked me to come with them," she said. "But I'm used to it here. I've lived in this city all my life. The kids say it's ugly and falling down, but I don't mind. These cracked old walls hold a lot of people who care about each other. In California, I'd just be another lonely blade of grass."

"How could you be grass? You're a person, not a plant."

"I'm getting so shriveled up, I'm more like a tough old vine than a human being." Miss Annie held out her arm. It was twisted and skinny.

"Vines can't talk."

"Maybe they talk at night, when you're sleeping."

"No, they don't."

"You seem awfully sure about things, Vernon." Her face was serious but her eyes were smiling. "How can you be so sure?"

It was hard to tell when she was joking. "From what I've seen, I guess," I said uneasily.

"If you were blind, would it be different?"

"I don't know. I guess it would be the same, but not for me, because I couldn't see it."

"Ahhhhh." Miss Annie nodded. "It would be different for *you*."

I squirmed in my chair. "Miss Annie, I have to go. I have other homework to do."

"Goodness, don't let me keep you from doing your homework." She looked at the big clock on her bookcase. "You *had* better go. You shouldn't let me ramble on." She handed me my notebook. "I'll see you tomorrow."

She could ramble, too; but she knew how to get what she wanted. After a couple of weeks she said, "Vernon, I've never asked you for money. I figured you didn't have any to spare. But I'd like you to pay for your tutoring another way: by working."

"What do you want me to do?"

"I'd like you to help Maxine clean up her yard. There are old boards and rags and papers all over the place. It bothers me every time I look at it."

"Uhhhh . . ." My face got red. I hadn't guessed she'd want me to help *Maxine*. What if the guys saw me there?

"I've mentioned it to her, but she and Ronald don't seem to get around to cleaning it up," Miss Annie continued. If she noticed the look on my face, she didn't let on. "But if you were to help, I know they'd get it done." She took out a little calendar. "Shall we set a date right now?"

Suddenly I thought of a way out. "What if I go down there and she's—you know . . . drunk?"

"Then we can set another date." Miss Annie was brisk. "How about Sunday afternoon, for starters?"

"I guess so."

"Wonderful. I'll tell Maxine two o'clock, all right?"

I nodded miserably.

"And I'll give her some trash bags," Miss Annie said cheerfully. She patted me on the arm. "I'm sure you'll get the job done quickly, a big strong boy like you."

"Thanks," I muttered.

"You may like them, once you get to know them," Miss Annie said.

I didn't say anything. I didn't even want to think about it.

"I'll see you tomorrow," Miss Annie said sweetly. "Keep up the good work."

7

I WENT DOWN THERE AFTER CHURCH. It was a sunny winter afternoon, but I pulled the drawstring tight on the hood of my parka, hoping no one would recognize me. Maybe Maxine wouldn't be home. I banged on her door. She opened it, smiling. Her lipstick was fluorescent orange. "Come in, Vernon," she said. "Ronald and I have been waiting for you."

"I'll just go ahead and do it real quick by myself," I said. But she shook her head.

"We couldn't leave you out there by yourself, after you've volunteered to help us. Here, sit down while we get our coats on."

Volunteered? My mouth opened, but I snapped it shut again. So Miss Annie hadn't told Maxine she was making me do the work. I felt kind of embarrassed. Then I saw what they were wearing. I looked away.

Ronald wasn't so bad: He had on regular pants and shoes, a ragged parka, a pink-striped scarf, and a red-and-blue-checked cap. One of his gloves was brown and the other was red. Maxine apologized for that: "Ronald and I just can't hold on to a pair of gloves," she said. "Luckily the Goodwill sells single ones for a nickel."

"Oh." The word sounded more like a prayer than anything else. I closed my eyes. Maybe I was hoping the good fairy would fly down and rescue me.

"Vernon?"

"Yes, ma'am?"

"We're ready."

I took a peek. My prayer had not been answered.

Maxine had put on a purple fake-fur coat with a red-striped belt around the waist. Her hat was black velvet, the kind old ladies wear to church, with a big gold pin on the front. Her gloves were yellow and pink, and she had a red plastic pocketbook over her arm.

"Uhhhh . . . you might not need the handbag."

She opened it wide. It was stuffed with trash bags. "Come on, Ronald," she said. "This is going to be fun."

The truth is, it wasn't as bad as I expected. Just stepping out the door with the two of them was the hardest part. I kept my hood up and ducked behind the hedge. If I worked like crazy, I might be out of there in forty-five minutes. I grabbed some boards and started stacking them beside the alley.

"What would you like me and Ronald to do?"

"Ummmm, why don't you pick up the empty pop bottles? And maybe Ronald can hold the trash bag open for you."

"Ronald, come here. Vernon has a special job for you."

Ronald shuffled over. Maxine produced a trash bag out of the pocketbook and showed him how to hold it. Then she began heaving stuff into it, bang, bang, bang. And the whole time she was talking.

"You're doing good, honey. Just keep that bag open wide. Why, we'll have this yard cleaned up in no time. Isn't he doing good, Vernon?"

"Yeah." I hauled more stuff over to the alley. I was starting to sweat with my hood up like it was. I undid the drawstring and eased it back from my face.

"Look at these McDonald's boxes. Who could have put them here? Ronald and I can't afford to eat at McDonald's."

I didn't say anything.

"Last night I made Ronald spaghetti. I made half a pound, and he ate every single bit of it. That's your favorite, isn't it, Ronald?"

I saw him nod. He was standing there holding that trash bag like it was the most important job on earth. Seeing him like that, trying so hard to do something so simple, gave me a funny feeling inside. I put more stuff over the fence.

"Back in North Carolina, us kids used to get so hungry

we'd steal from the neighbor's garden. We'd dig sweet potatoes and take them out in the woods and roast them. They'd smell so good, we could hardly wait till they got soft. To this day I love the smell of yams."

My mother used to cook yams for Thanksgiving. I hadn't thought about that for a while, the way the kitchen was with the turkey and cornbread and yam smells coming out of the oven all at once. I swallowed. "They do smell good," I said.

We got it done in a little over an hour. At the end you'd have thought I was the captain of a *Mission: Impossible* team from the way she talked.

"Vernon," she said, "Ronald and I wouldn't have known where to begin without you."

"That's all right."

"We've lived here five years, and this is as good as this yard has ever looked."

I nodded.

"Come March I might try to put in a little garden, now that those boards are gone. I just might."

I nodded. "We'll see you soon," Maxine said. "Stop on down whenever you feel like it." She went up the steps, around the hole in the porch floor, and into the house, with Ronald holding on behind her.

8

B Y NOW MOST OF THE KIDS KNEW I was going to Miss Annie's to be tutored. I guess they didn't know whether to laugh or feel sorry for me. They tried a little of both. Like a couple of times Bobby said, "Going down to see your girlfriend, Vern?"

I smiled and said, "Yep."

Another time I heard Chris tell them, "Vern's getting his grade up in English. Looks like he's going to squeak by, after all."

But the kids didn't know I knew Maxine. Of course, I was hoping they wouldn't find out.

"If you could just stay with Ronald for an hour, Maxine would be able to buy her food stamps," Miss Annie said after my lesson. "What do you say? You could work on those grammar exercises I gave you."

What *could* I say? I nodded.

"Good. I'll tell her you're coming right now."

It turned out Ronald didn't want to be with me any more than I wanted to be with him. When he saw Maxine getting her coat on, he jumped up and grabbed her arm. He looked at her and he looked at me and then he looked back at her. You would have thought I was an ax murderer.

"You remember Vernon," Maxine said. "He helped us clean up the yard."

Ronald whined.

"Now don't fuss, Ronald—be a big boy. I won't be gone long. *Mickey Mouse Club* and *Lassie* are on TV. Vernon will change the channel for you."

Ronald looked like he was going to cry. Maxine went over and opened the refrigerator. She pulled out one of those jumbo plastic bottles of Shasta. There was just a little bit in it. Ronald pointed.

"I'm going to fix it for you," she said. "And Vernon, too, if he wants some."

"No, thanks."

I watched her pour the soda into a jelly glass and put a cube of ice in it. She gave it to Ronald. "Now be good," she said. She kissed him on the forehead and left.

Be good? I wondered if Ronald knew how to be bad. His eyes darted from side to side, avoiding me. He gripped the glass tight. I was disgusted. Did he think

I'd take his dumb soda?

"I don't want it," I said curtly. Then I said something mean. "I don't want to be with you, either. I'm only here because Miss Annie made me come."

Ronald moaned out loud. His eyes were racing back and forth.

"Just watch Mickey Mouse and be quiet," I said.

Ronald moaned louder. He looked at the door. I wondered if he was about to make a run for it. If he got out before I caught him, he'd probably go right straight to Miss Annie's. Then she'd know I'd messed up. Maybe she'd refuse to tutor me anymore. I tried to think. Suddenly I remembered a trick I used to do for my little cousins.

"Hey, Ronald," I said. "I can make money disappear."

He must have noticed a change in my voice, because he stopped moaning and looked at me. I took a quarter out of my pocket and held it up. I hid it between the crack in my fingers and pretended to pull it out of his ear. He jerked his head away, but he couldn't stop staring at the money. I could see the question in his eyes.

"Want me to do it again?"

He jerked his head up and down.

"Here it is, see? And now it's gone." He bent over, looking at my empty hand. "Now I'll make it come back." I put my hand by his ear. "One, two, three— presto!"

Ronald's mouth fell open. He looked at me, and he looked at the money. I could tell he wanted me to do it

41

again. That was funny—I hadn't known someone could talk without words.

"Last time." I showed him the quarter. He put his face so close, he actually touched the money with his nose. I pointed out the window to distract him while I hid it, and then I made it come out his nose. He was so surprised, he jumped. I had to stop myself from laughing.

"Time for Mickey Mouse."

He must have seen that lots of times, because he bobbed his head in time to the music, and when each of those little twerps came out onstage, he looked sort of pleased and excited, as if he'd been waiting for them. But now and then he looked at me. His eyes were doubtful and curious and scared.

After a while he forgot about the trick. He finished watching Mickey Mouse and I turned on *Lassie* like Maxine had said to. He really got into it. That was when I noticed the change.

You see, when you first saw Ronald, he looked like an ugly animal that got on this earth somehow and really shouldn't have. I mean, there wasn't a single part of him that was nice-looking. His arms and legs were too long, and his body was as skinny as a fence post. His face had acne, and his eyes bulged, and his mouth wouldn't hold still.

But what I figured out was, a lot of Ronald's problem was fear. He was scared of everything and everybody, and being scared made him gawky and pop-eyed and crazy-looking. Because sitting there watching *Lassie*, he forgot about me. Then he wasn't so bad-looking after all. In fact, he looked pretty much like a regular teenager—not good-looking, but not awful, either.

I figured out that Ronald knew more than he let on. Like near the end of the show, when this rattlesnake hid under a rock near Timmy and Lassie, Ronald knew that was dangerous. He grunted and pointed to the rock, like he was trying to warn them. Then he looked at me. I could see he was asking, would I help? It was like he was the kid and I was the grown-up.

"The snake won't bite Lassie or Timmy," I explained. I kept my voice even, like a teacher would. "Because if the snake bit them, they'd die, and the show would go off the air."

Ronald's eyes were big. He was still worried.

"I used to watch this show every week when I was a kid. Believe me, Lassie never gets hurt bad. She's the star of the show, so they have to keep her in good shape."

Just then the sheriff rode up in a Jeep, shot the snake, and threw it down a ravine. Ronald sighed and sat back. Lassie came running out.

"You see, there she is. Just like I told you, she's fine."

Ronald looked over. His mouth twitched, but there was something different about this twitching. I was pretty sure he was trying to smile.

I meant to be out of there as soon as Maxine got

back. She tried to get me to stay for supper. She'd stopped by the store on the way home and bought a tray of chicken wings. "I can make some good fried chicken," she said. "Ronald's daddy taught me that."

"His daddy?"

She nodded as if she hadn't said anything unusual. "W. B. Swan, his name is. He learned to cook down in Carolina when he was a little boy."

I guess I must have been staring, 'cause she laughed. "Everybody's got a daddy, Vernon. You're old enough to know that."

"I just never thought . . ." My voice died.

"No, we didn't get married, and he ain't been around too much the last ten years. But he's a good soul."

I got hold of myself. "Did the two of you move up here together?"

"No, honey." She smiled, but she wasn't looking at me. Her hands moved automatically, dipping the chicken pieces in flour, shaking them off. "I came up here to be a government secretary near the end of World War II. They had a labor shortage back then, so it didn't matter if you didn't have a lot of schooling. I was dirt-poor when I left Carolina, but within a month I was making twenty-one dollars a week. I was even sending a little bit home to my brothers and sisters. And I bought makeup and pretty dresses and high heels—I was in heaven!" She sighed. "Then the war ended. They closed the building down, and all of us had to find new jobs."

"Is that when you met W. B.?"

"Mercy, no. There were lots of others before him."
She chuckled. "I always liked him specially though,
'cause he was from Carolina. He was a good dresser,
and he loved to party. He could drink all night and go
to work in the morning like a new man." She looked up
suddenly. "Sure you won't have some of this chicken,
Vernon?"

"No, thanks. My family's probably waiting on me
right now."

"We'll see you later, then."

I nodded. I said good-bye to Ronald, put my coat on,
and hurried out the door.

9

"BOBBY WAS LOOKING FOR YOU," my little brother said at supper. "He came up here three times."

"What did he want?"

Ben shrugged. "Don't ask me. I told him you was probably down at the teacher's, or else at the crazy lady's."

I glared. "Why'd you tell him that?"

"What?"

"That I was down there. And you shouldn't be calling her that, either."

He ignored that part. "You been down there sometimes."

"How do you know?"

"Mitchell told me. He seen you down there, cleaning up her yard."

46

"Mitchell needs to mind his own beeswax. And so do you."

Ben looked down at his plate. His face started getting red.

"You don't need to holler at him, Vern," Steph said. Tony nodded, like he was my boss too.

"You stay out of it." I glared at Tony. "Ben shouldn't be telling my friends I'm here, there, and everywhere when he doesn't even know what he's talking about."

"Do too," Ben muttered. His hand was tight around his fork.

"Do not. And tell your dumb little friends to stop spying on me, you hear?"

"Mitchell ain't dumb! He's smart as you are."

Everybody looked up then. I felt my scalp getting hot.

"Mitchell don't even got the sense to tie his own shoes. Runs around tripping on his shoelaces."

"Does not!" Ben jumped up quick, like he was going to take a poke at me. I guess he thought better of it, 'cause he's scrawny as a half-starved cat. Then Daddy stood up. He went over and pulled Ben's chair out, like he was in some fancy restaurant. "Have a seat, Benjy." Ben flopped back down, but a minute later I noticed tears splashing down his face. I could have said something mean, but I didn't, 'cause Daddy was looking at me.

"You cleaned her yard up?" he asked.

"Who?" I didn't want to talk about it, I can tell you.

"Maxine Flooter."

I nodded.

"You didn't charge her for it, did you, son?"

"No."

"Why'd you do it, then?" somebody asked.

"'Cause I wanted to."

"Wish you'd clean up our yard, Vernon. There's a hole in the back fence, and Mrs. Potter's cats keep coming in and doing their business in the flower garden." That was Steph.

"Vernon doesn't even hang around here," Ben said. He was still sniffling. "Soon as he gets home, he goes down on the next block. He won't even play catch."

Everybody looked at me again. I shrugged. "I been busy."

"I'm your brother, but you don't care nothing about me." Ben pulled a long face.

"I care," Tony said. He winked at Ben. "I'm coming home early to play ball with you tomorrow. The lab is closed for a teacher conference, so I can't stay late."

"You're coming early for real?"

Tony nodded.

"Hot dog!" Ben said. "I'll be here!"

"Hot dog!" I mimicked his reedy voice till Steph gave me a look that said be quiet. I scowled at my plate. Nobody had stuck up for me. They hadn't even asked why I'd been late. Maybe I'd have been better off eating with Maxine and Ronald, after all.

48

That night I couldn't sleep. The light in the hall was off, the way it usually is when everyone's in bed, so I felt my way downstairs. A radio was playing softly in the kitchen. I poked my head in. Daddy was sitting in the dark at the kitchen table, his head resting on one hand. He must have been half asleep, 'cause he jumped when he saw me.

"Vern!" he whispered. "What are you doing up?"

"I was hungry."

"I'll make you something."

"I can do it myself," I said stiffly. I still felt mad from suppertime.

"No, I'd like to." He got up, opened the refrigerator door, and poked around. "There's bologna in here, and yellow cheese . . ."

"Steph bought that stuff for school lunches."

"Uh-oh. Maybe it better be jelly, then."

He made the sandwich in the dark, humming along with the song on the radio. "The Everly Brothers," he said when it was over. "Nineteen fifty-eight." He slid the plate in front of me. "Want a glass of milk?"

"Sure."

"Here." He sat down then. His face was almost as pale as his white T-shirt. "So you cleaned her yard up," he said.

I nodded. My mouth was stuffed with bread and jelly.

"Mary always liked her—she made her boy a coat

49

one time. She used to say when Maxine was sober she had more sense than the president and the pope combined." He laughed a little, then brushed his hand across his eyes. "All the memories," he murmured.

I waited until I'd finished my mouthful. "Why does she drink?"

Daddy shrugged. "I don't know. She worked on the line out at Sweetheart Cup for years along with your Aunt Barb. They said she used to drink back then, but she hardly ever missed a day. I'd see her now and then when I picked Barb up. Then they automated the plant, and everybody on the line got laid off. They let go people who had fifteen and twenty years with the company. Some of them were bitter. The life insurance, pension, everything they'd set aside for their families went right out the window."

"She could have got another job."

"That's like saying you can get another husband after the first one runs off and leaves you. There's a lot of hurt you have to go through first."

I poured myself another glass of milk. "She never married Ronald's dad," I said.

If he disapproved, he didn't say so. "Seems like she's used to doing things her own way."

"Her way can be nuts, Dad. The other day she screamed at the mailman for bringing her a welfare check—'I don't want no government money!' Then she remembered she had to pay her oil bill, so she ran up the street and hollered at him to give it back. He was so disgusted, he almost threw the mailbag at her."

Daddy chuckled. "I'll bet the mailman was Pete Danilowski. He's always been a little high and mighty. If she took him down a peg, that's all right with me."

"But she didn't. She just ended up looking stupid."

"Maybe stupid, but more likely practical." He folded his hands together. They were smaller than my hands, but strong-looking. "Sometimes Maxine says things the rest of us would like to say but can't, because of our jobs and our children."

"But she has Ronald."

"That's why she went back after the check. And another day—say she'd had too much to drink—she might not have gone back. Then Ronald would have had to suffer the consequences."

What consequences? I wondered. I thought of the two of them sitting with their platter of chicken wings hot on the table, the TV buzzing comfortably behind them. And I thought of our supper, the hurt feelings flying back and forth like spitballs in a schoolbus. "Did you ever wish you didn't have so many kids?" I asked Daddy.

He looked startled. "No, Vernon, I didn't," he said. "In fact sometimes we used to wish we had a couple more."

"A couple more!"

Daddy laughed. "We didn't know what was good for us, I guess. But each of you was so different, kind of like a surprise package that kept changing, getting better." His voice faded, as if remembering had taken his strength away. Suddenly I felt tired too.

"Thanks for the sandwich."

"Sure."

"Aren't you going to bed, Daddy?"

"In a minute. I'm just going to listen to one more song."

They put on Elvis as I left. I heard Daddy singing with him as I went upstairs in the dark.

10

MAXINE WAS DRUNK again.

Two days running she came up the middle of the block with Ronald on her arm. She was hollering and cussing like there was no tomorrow. I hid up on the porch but she saw me anyway.

"Vernon," she hollered. "How you?"

I didn't answer.

"You too proud to talk to Maxine? You better talk! If you don't, the president's going to shoot you with a poison arrow!"

I laughed. She laughed, too.

"You're a good boy, Vernon," she shouted. "One day you'll be an angel up in heaven. God will set a golden crown on your head."

She went on up the street, with Ronald behind her.

———

But in the next couple of weeks she got it together, or so I thought. I kept going to Miss Annie's for tutoring, and twice she asked me to do things for Maxine: simple stuff like setting her trash out in the alley and helping her turn Ronald's mattress. Each time, Maxine told me more about them: how the doctors in the newborn wing had told her Ronald would never be able to walk or feed himself, and how she'd fought to keep him with her even though they thought he should be put in a state hospital. Just after that she got the job at Sweetheart Cup.

"I had to prove I could provide for Ronald, and I did. They used to say I was the fastest one on the assembly line. When they laid us off, my boss like to cried. 'You been one of the best out here, Maxine,' he said. 'After all these years, it hurts to let you go.'"

"What happened then?"

She shrugged, as if it really didn't matter. "I drew unemployment for a while, but that wasn't enough to pay for Ronald's and my apartment, so we had to move into a charity hotel. Then somebody from the Holiness Mission found us this house and gave us the first month's rent. She asked me to get down on my knees and thank Jesus, but I said I'd rather thank her. I was raised a Baptist, but they're too holy for me now. When I go to church, I go to St. Francis."

"I never saw you there."

"Me and Ronald go to early mass." A light came into her eye. "What mass do you go to, Vernon?"

I wished I hadn't brought it up. "Ten thirty, or sometimes noon, if we're running late."

"Maybe I'll see you there on Sunday."

"Yeah, maybe."

"Would you like a biscuit? They just came out of the oven."

"Don't mind if I do."

Me and Ronald cleaned those biscuits up, and a bowl of black-eyed peas and some cole slaw to boot. Ronald could almost outeat me. He'd gotten more comfortable around me, too. Sometimes he'd pull on my shirt sleeve to get me to do the money trick. He showed me how he could get Brownie to jump up in his lap just by patting his leg with his hand. He was proud of that. Once I gave him a candy bar. He held that thing like it was gold.

I didn't see Maxine for a few days, but I did see Bobby, and he said they'd seen her on the street, drunk as the devil. At first I thought he might be saying it just to get to me. But it turned out he wasn't, 'cause when I went down to Miss Annie's, her tutoring books were lying closed on the table.

"I've got something more important for you to do," she said.

"What?"

"The police picked Maxine up a couple of nights ago. They've got her in the lockup at Central—she's been sentenced to ten days for D&D. Do you know what that is?"

"Drunk and disorderly?"

She nodded. She paused for a minute, to let it sink in. "I want you to go down there today," she said. "I have a message for her. I'd go myself, but my arthritis is too bad."

I just stood there.

"Tell her I got her welfare and disability checks from her mailbox. If she'll sign them, I'll get Jean Snyder to cash them and get a money order for her rent. Tell her Ronald is fine. He's at school now, and the neighbors and I will take care of him until she gets home. Tell her we're thinking of her. And give her this." She handed me a box of oatmeal cookies. "Now tell me the message back."

I did.

"Good, Vernon. You have a fine memory." She patted me on the shoulder. "You know how to get down there?"

I nodded.

"Here's money for the bus. When you get back, bring me the checks right away. It's not safe to keep them in your pocket too long. Good-bye now."

On my way up the hill I thought about not going. All I had to do was put the checks in Miss Annie's mailbox and walk home, and I'd be free of all three of them. With the extra work I'd done in tutoring, I had a decent chance of passing English right now. I'd never promised them anything, none of them.

I kept walking, thinking. People were lined up at the bus stop on the corner. I hung back, checking out the windows of the shoe stores and clothing shops. The bus was huffing our way, its brakes squealing like the kid at the bottom of the pile in a playground fight. I remembered Ben used to have a bus with a string on the front. He'd pulled that thing up and down the sidewalk till he'd almost worn a groove in the cement. I stood behind the others, waiting my turn, thinking that something was pulling me, too. I hesitated on the steps. The driver looked at me: "Well?" He had a thin face, worn and sad-looking. I got on the bus.

The women's jail is an ugly concrete building. They took me to the visiting section, which was gray and light green with flaking paint. There were five little glass windows with bars and screens across them, and telephones hanging beside them. After a few minutes the guard brought Maxine in, and she sat down behind one of the windows.

I had never seen her look so bad. She was wearing a baggy dress with a number on the pocket. Her hair was hanging around her neck in long strings, and her skin looked gray. She didn't smile; she hardly opened her eyes to look at me.

I picked up the phone to tell her the message.

"It's broke," the guard said. "They're all broke. You have to shout."

I yelled it through. I couldn't hand her the checks; I had to give them to the guard, who looked at them and took them around and brought them back. She wouldn't give Maxine the cookies right away. She said they had to be inspected first.

"Tell Ronald I'll be home soon," Maxine said. She said it so low I could hardly hear.

"I will."

We sat there for a moment longer. I wanted to leave but not with her looking like that. I couldn't think of anything to say. Then I reached into my pocket and happened to feel the bus fare that was left.

"I'm going to buy Ronald a soda on the way home," I said. "What kind does he like?"

For a minute I thought she hadn't heard. Then I saw her lips move: "Orange Crush."

I got up to leave. The guard fastened a handcuff on Maxine's wrist and started to lead her away. She looked back at me, and her lips moved again. I think she said, "Thank you, Vernon."

I walked home so I could spend the bus fare on soda. At the end I stopped at the A&P and got it.

"It's for Ronald," I told Miss Annie.

"How nice of you," she said. "He's in the other room. Why don't you give it to him?"

He was surprised to see me. I acted like a magician and pulled out the soda: "Poof!" But instead of reaching for it, he turned his back.

"What's the matter? I thought this was your favorite."

58

He looked out the window like I wasn't there. Then I understood.

"She'll be home soon. She told me to tell you."

He kept standing there, not looking at me. Finally I unscrewed the top of the soda and took it around to him. "She said for you to drink it," I lied.

He took it then, but his eyes were hurt. I sat down, and after a while he came and sat beside me. I wondered how old he was—probably only a couple of years older than me. His hair was brown, like mine, and he was tall, maybe even the tallest in his class. And he missed his mom. I swallowed. Two boys, I thought, alike and not alike, both missing their mothers.

I got home in time for supper. They were sitting around the table, all of them. If they wondered where I'd been, they didn't ask, maybe because of what I'd said about minding your own business. That was funny, because all of a sudden I wanted to tell about this afternoon, and how I'd felt with Ronald. I didn't know where to begin. Then Steph said, "Pass your plate for the meat loaf, Vern. Sandra made it, and it's good."

"Mitchell's got a tire," Ben said. "He found it down the alley. There's an inch of tread on part of it."

"Good meat loaf," Daddy said. He was watching the news.

"He's gonna sell it," Ben said. "And if he gets a dollar, he'll give me fifty cents."

"I've got three fifty saved up," Sandra said. "I'm saving for Crystal Barbie."

"You should ask for it for your birthday. Then you can spend the three fifty on ice cream. We can split it." Ben smiled.

"Anything new, Vern?" Steph asked. Our eyes met.

I wanted to tell them, but it was already too late. The words were stuck somewhere under the meat loaf and potatoes, on the other side of Crystal Barbie and a worn-out tire. I shook my head.

11

A FEW DAYS LATER I GOT MY MIDTERM grades for the second semester. I'd held the C in shop and gym, brought Earth Sciences and English up to a C–, and kept a D in math. I had the F in French, but of course I knew that was coming. My English teacher put a note beside my mark: "Much improvement." I breathed a sigh of relief.

The guys were ragging me: "When you going to take your head out of the books, huh, Vern? You turning into an egghead?"

They had spring fever, and I did, too. It was hard to sit still, even to stand still. Miss Annie noticed.

"Maybe you'd like to take a few days off, Vernon. You've been working hard."

I just stood there. I wanted to, all right.

"Go ahead," she said. "Come back on Monday. The

rest will probably do you good."

I wouldn't exactly say I rested over that week. I got together with the guys, and I'd say we were feeling the same thing: like we were waiting for something to happen. I didn't know what or where or when, but there was that feeling.

We played a bunch of games of pickup ball. We took apart the engine of a junked car that had been sitting in Jerry's backyard. We walked all the way up to Rosedale to try to see this girl that Bobby had said was more beautiful than Farrah Fawcett. When we got there, none of us had the nerve to knock on her door, so we just stood around on the sidewalk, hoping she'd come out. She didn't, though.

I made up with Milt. I saw him on the sidewalk, getting into his LTD, and he said, "We haven't seen your family around for quite a while. Where've you been?"

"We've been here," I said. "Guess we've just been going to the A&P. Prices are lower up there."

"Prices are lower, but it's a long walk up that hill," Milt said. "You come by and see us sometime, and I'll give you a soda."

I didn't say anything.

"I always did like your daddy," Milt said. "You come on by and get a soda, on me."

Maxine got out of jail. I didn't see her right away, but Ben's friend Mitchell told me she was back. I asked,

"Was she sober?"

He shrugged. "She wasn't cussing, but she had on a pair of red sunglasses, the kind with mirrors in them. And Ronald had on a blue pair."

"Where'd you see them?"

"Going up the hill."

Uh-oh, I thought, I'd better go down later and see how they are. But I forgot I'd told Jerry I'd work on his ten-speed. The gears were so messed up, it wouldn't even go. I spent the whole evening over there fiddling with it. We never did get it straightened out.

The next day I got a surprise. There was a note for me in our mailbox when I got home from school.

> Vernon Dibbs,
> Could you come down tomorrow at 4 p.m.
> Ronald's teacher is coming for a home visit. I
> want her to meet you.
> Maxine

I went down early to make sure things were okay. I could hardly believe my eyes. The house was neat and Maxine was dressed like a normal person, in plaid slacks and a brown sweater. Ronald was sitting at the kitchen table, and Brownie was tied up in the backyard with a big bowl of dog food beside him. I plunked myself down next to Ronald.

"What's the visit for?" I asked. "None of my teachers come to my house."

"That's 'cause you're not special, like Ronald." She brushed his hair into place with one hand. "They have to make sure he's taken care of right."

"Do they know about last week?"

"What about last week?"

"You being—you know—in jail."

Maxine glared. "Forget about that, would you? All they know is what they see today. And that's all those busybodies need to know."

"You can't talk like that when she comes."

"Vernon Dibbs, I know what to say and what not to say."

"I hope so."

Someone knocked at the door. Maxine went to answer it. I was kidding around with Ronald. I heard their voices outside, and then they came into the kitchen. My mouth dropped open, because there was Ronald's teacher, and if ever a woman deserved the name beautiful, it was her.

"I'm Miss Marlow," she said in a soft voice. She put out her hand. When I touched it, I started sweating.

"Ver . . . Vernon Dibbs," I stuttered.

Ronald liked her too. He stood up and stepped from one foot to the other, back and forth.

"Sit down, Ronald," Maxine said. "I'll get you all some soda." She came back with four glasses. She put them on the table and sat down herself.

"Ronald has had such a good year," Miss Marlow started. "His attendance has been excellent, and he's

worked very hard. He's mastered several new skills."
She told us what they were.

"One reason we make these home visits is to make
sure that the parents—or parent"—she looked at Maxine apologetically—"know what our focus is and are
working along with us at home. We like to be certain
that a child's home life is adequate to meet his needs.
After all, when we talk about children like Ronald,
we're talking about very special children."

I shifted in my seat.

"I don't have a lot of money to buy things for
Ronald," Maxine said. "But he gets enough to eat. He
eats like a horse."

"Not everyone can be affluent," Miss Marlow said.

"Ronald has things to do, and he has friends, too,"
Maxine said. "He watches shows on TV. And Vernon
here is one of his friends."

I turned red.

"Do you ever get the chance to take Ronald to extra
activities, like an exercise class? Gymnastics clubs are
offering all kinds of courses for the retarded, and some
YMCAs are too. Not everyone is aware that these
things are available."

"I don't have a car," Maxine said. I could feel she was
getting agitated. "When Ronald and I go somewhere,
we have to walk or take the bus."

"The Special Olympics is going to be held at the university only a mile from here in June. There will be out-
door activities for someone like Ronald. It's a lot of fun."

"Would he need anything special for it?" Maxine looked doubtful.

"Nothing but a pair of tennis shoes," Miss Marlow said. "And an assistant to help him. You, or anyone you choose."

Maxine didn't say anything. I knew she was wondering where she'd get the money to buy Ronald tennis shoes.

"It would be so good for him," Miss Marlow said. "He'd be a part of something that was for people just like him. And it's close by, too."

"I'll go with him," I said. I had a feeling somebody needed to say that.

"That's wonderful, Vernon." Miss Marlow smiled right at me. She seemed to relax a little, and she checked off something in her notebook. "I'll send a sign-up form here. Maxine can give it to you, and you can fill it out."

"Okay."

She stood up. Ronald jumped up too. She put her hand on his arm gently.

"You're going to stay here now, but I'll see you in school tomorrow morning. Understand?"

He nodded.

"I'm glad I could come and see you, Ronald," she said. She waved, and he waved right back at her.

12

I COULD HARDLY SIT STILL that night. Daddy was working the late shift, so it was just us kids. The conversation was going back and forth about something on the news: President Reagan said one thing, Congress said another. Steph stood with the Congress but Tony thought the president had the right idea. Ben and Sandra were giggling over a beat-up copy of *Mad* magazine. The blood was pulsing through my head: Miss Marlow, tennis shoes, Maxine, Miss Marlow, over and over like the rhythm to a song.

"Vern, you hardly touched your meat," Steph said. "Are you sick?"

"No."

"He turned into a vegetabletarian," Ben said.

"Vegetarian," Tony corrected him.

"Did you?" Sandra looked at me like I'd changed

overnight into somebody different.

"Of course not. I'm not hungry, is all."

"You *must* be sick."

"No. I just got things on my mind."

"What kind of things?"

"Like . . ." I hesitated. I hadn't meant to tell them, but it came out; not everything, but enough: that Maxine had asked me to be there when Miss Marlow came; what she'd said; and how I'd volunteered to take Ronald to the Special Olympics.

"You should have kept your mouth shut," Tony said. "Now you're going to have to get him a pair of tennis shoes."

"How much do you think they'll cost?"

"Twenty-five dollars. I priced them at Shoe City just the other day."

"I don't have that kind of money."

"Me neither," Steph said. But I could see she was thinking. After a minute she said, "Maybe you could have a bake sale for Ronald. I'll bet people on the block would give cakes."

"Etta might make a pie," Sandra said. "Her sweet potato pie is good."

"I'd buy a piece of that," Tony said. "Ask her."

Then I had an idea. It hit me hard, like an old car banging into a cinder-block wall. I held on to it for a minute, just to make sure there wasn't anything wrong with it.

"Remember years ago . . . back when Mom was alive,

we used to send away for those kits where you set up a little carnival in your backyard? And you'd make ten or eleven dollars, and give it all to charity?"

"Muscular dystrophy," Steph said. "I remember."

"Well, why couldn't I do something like that for Ronald? Not just me, but the whole block?"

There was silence at the table. Tony raised his eyebrows. "Sounds like a pretty big job," he said. "Who would run it?"

I knew what he was getting at: that I'd screw it up, like I did my schoolwork. My fists clenched under the table, but I kept my voice steady. "I would."

"Do you think you could handle it? I mean, you've been pretty busy with your tutoring."

"I can do it," I said coldly. "I have a week off at Easter."

"But there're a lot of decisions that go into something like that, Vern. And the profits have to be collected and added up. Nothing personal, but you're not exactly a math whiz."

"Don't tell me what I am and what I'm not!" I was starting to sweat. "I said I can do it, and I can."

Tony shrugged, like it didn't matter anyway. Steph tried to break the mood. "Those carnivals were a lot of fun," she said. "I remember Mom used to make up all kinds of goofy contests. Once I stood on my head for eight minutes. I've never been the same since."

Everybody laughed then, and somehow I knew it was okay to go ahead with it. I couldn't help thinking if

Mom were here, she'd do it. And that made me all the more determined to make it happen.

It seems like I wasn't the only one who had spring fever. Once the idea of the carnival for Ronald got out, the block jumped on it like a rat on cheese. I could hardly walk up the street without somebody coming out to tell me they'd make cookies or type up announcements or sell hot dogs. A guy who was an usher at the stadium said he'd get all the players to sign a baseball for us, and we could raffle it off. And Daddy came up with a great idea. Around here a lot of people spend the whole weekend underneath their car. Daddy said if those guys volunteered to do tune-ups and compression checks and oil changes and give us the profits, we'd be flush.

There was only one hang-up in this whole thing: I hadn't told the guys about it yet. I didn't want to tell them. For one thing, they didn't know I'd actually become friends with Maxine and Ronald. For another, the idea seemed goody-goody, the kind of thing you'd do if you were a little kid or a grown-up, but not someone in between. They were going to say I was turning into a nerd.

I worried about that: not just that they'd say it but that it might be true. I stared at my face in the mirror. I don't wear glasses, or bow ties, or get my hair cut in bangs across the front; if you saw me, you'd think *normal*. But was I? It was okay for girls to want to do well at school, but not for boys; they weren't supposed to care. Liking people like Ronald and Maxine and Miss Annie was pretty strange, too. And deciding to help them? I looked into my eyes. I half expected this weird little bald guy to pop out and start waving at me, like he was my true self. He didn't, though. I sighed. I decided to skip tutoring for the day. Instead I went down around the corner and drove some finishing nails into Mr. Ward's rear tires. Mr. Ward hates kids. Every baseball that's ever rolled into his yard, he's got someplace inside that house. When he dies, we're going to get them back.

In the end, I lied to the guys. I said I'd been down at Miss Annie's getting tutored, and when I'd come out the door, I'd seen this beautiful woman. She looked so sad, I asked her what was wrong. She told me Ronald didn't have enough money to get tennis shoes for the Special Olympics. She was his teacher, and she really wanted him to go. Did I know anybody who could help?

For a minute my mind was blank. Then suddenly I'd remembered way back when we were kids, how we used to throw those little fairs in our backyards. I'd held back for a bit, thinking she might laugh at the idea, but she looked as if she was about to cry. So I'd mentioned it. She grabbed my hands. "Vernon, would you?" she said. How could I turn her down?

Bobby squinted at me. "If you knew his size, you

71

could rip the shoes off," he said. "That would be a lot quicker. And I'd cover for you."

"But I don't know his size," I pointed out. I wasn't going to say that ripping off a pair of tennis shoes would be a lot harder than stealing a candy bar.

"What did she look like?" Jerry asked. "Was she blond?"

I told him.

They guys shook their heads and laughed. Maybe they guessed I was bullshitting. They didn't volunteer to help, but they didn't put me down either. I breathed a sigh of relief.

But later—maybe a couple of days later—I got the surprise of my life. I was sitting out on the porch steps by myself, and Jerry came along and sat on the step just below me. He put down a little rock, and he was batting it back and forth between his shoes. After a while he said, "Know what, Vern?"

"What?"

"You know my brother Chuckie? And my brother Lewis?"

"Yeah." I guess I did—I'd known them all my life.

"Well, in between them, I've got another brother. Hardly anybody knows about him. He lives in a place like a hospital over on the west side. You know how I'm always gone when you guys play ball after church? That's 'cause we visit him then."

Jerry's voice sounded like it was all dried up. I just sat there. I couldn't believe my ears.

72

"He's like Ronald," Jerry said. "You know, retarded. But he's a real nice kid."

"What's his name?"

"John." Jerry cleared his throat. "He went to the Special Olympics last year. I didn't get to go with him. But when I went to see him afterward, he had three big old medals hanging on the wall over his bed. It was the biggest thing that ever happened to him, just about."

We sat there for a while longer. Jerry didn't speak and I didn't either. He batted that rock back and forth, and finally he got up. "Don't tell nobody," he said.

13

MISS ANNIE HELPED ME WITH the carnival. Together we wrote letters for the permits that let you block off the street. We made lists of what needed to be done, and who had to do it. She checked my spelling and made sure I had the commas and colons where they were supposed to be. "Clear writing and good thinking go together," she said, frowning at the crumpled papers I'd pull out of my back pocket. "Take the time to do this neatly and correctly."

"But I don't *have* time!"

"Yes, you do. You have a full two weeks before the fair. Now sit down with your pen and paper and get started."

I told Maxine about it ahead of time, which was a mistake. She was so excited she got drunk twice. She came flying down the street hollering that she was Jesus and we'd tour heaven Friday and she'd ask the Lord to give us all a free carnival cruise to Bermuda when we got back home. The second time she got dressed up in this spotted dress with a straw hat like a Mexican sombrero. "I'm married to Trini Lopez," she shouted. "He's going to come to the fair and sing for Ronald. He isn't Ronald's father, but he loves him anyway."

"You're not married to nobody, Maxine," a little girl said.

"Yes, I am." Maxine kind of shrugged her shoulders, like she was proud. "I'm married to myself!"

When the day came I was nervous. Daddy helped me lug folding tables from the parish hall and set them up. We brought out our old stereo for music and blew up some balloons. Then Ben and Mitchell surprised me with a banner they'd painted down in the basement. It showed some kids in wheelchairs and said "Help Send Ronald to the Special Olympics!" Jerry's dad got a stepladder and strung it up between two lampposts. It looked great.

Just about then the food started coming: cakes and cookies and pies and brownies and fudge on the bake tables; steamed crabs and chicken and greens and sweet potatoes in front of Mrs. Henry's; hot dogs and candy apples and sloppy joe on a bun and soda and Hawaiian Punch. Then up the street came Clarice Moore with a sheet cake decorated with a picture of a kid wearing an Olympic medal around his neck.

The entertainment was fine. Steph ran games for the little kids: relays, sack races, and a three-legged race. Then we had a dancing contest, which cost a dollar to enter. We raffled off the autographed baseball. About that time Milt came around the corner and gave us half a ham to auction off. People's chins just about fell down to their knees.

There were a couple of moments I'll never forget. One was in the afternoon. We'd been hearing all day that some big stars were coming to Tenley Heights to put on a show at three o'clock. Some of the kids believed it, and they were trying to figure out who it would be: Tom Selleck? Farrah Fawcett? I heard one little kid saying it was Big Bird. Jerry and I about busted a gut on that one.

Anyway, as the time got close, Chris Murphy came out of his house and started taking people's money. If you paid a dollar, you got to sit on the sidewalk in front of his porch, and if you paid fifty cents you got to sit in the street. I asked him what it was about. "Stay cool, dude," he said.

Then right at three his mother came out on the porch. She was dressed in a red-silk gown, with black net stockings and the highest heels I've ever laid eyes on. She had a microphone, and she started talking into it real sexy, saying she had something special for all of us, a package that had flown here all the way from California. Then she screamed, "And here they are! The Pointer Sisters!"

It took everybody a minute to figure it out. The three of them were perfect:

> *"I'm so excited . . .*
> *I just can't hide it,*
> *I'm about to lose control . . ."*

Their legs came forward together, with their high heels pointing straight out. Then somebody yelled, "It's Ralph Murphy!" and we saw one of them start to grin. Sure enough, it was Chris's dad with a wig and makeup and falsies and a blue evening gown. And right next to him was Lance Summers, who works for the post office, and the third one was some guy we didn't know. They were singing in these high voices that sounded like women. And they were good, too. Then Ralph's left boob started to slip. He got this shy expression, and he reached over and held it in place for the rest of the concert. I laughed so hard, Daddy had to pull me up out of the street when the thing was over.

"You know, Vern," he said, after I caught my breath, "I haven't seen Maxine."

"She told Mrs. Moore she and Ronald would be up later."

"I expect so." He looked around. "The neighborhood really came out for Ronald. And it's all your doing. You should be proud of yourself."

I should have known, the way the fair was going so

well, that something bad was about to happen. But like a dummy, I just kept on expecting the best. And for a while it did get better and better. For instance, Frank Gilberti put on a puppet show. That doesn't sound like much, I guess, except that he and his wife have lived across the street for a long, long time. They came here from Italy when they were young. They're nice, but he's the kind of guy who screams at you for dropping a gum wrapper on the ground. Their yard has a flower garden with little statues in between the flowers, and it has to be perfect.

Anyway, he came out on his porch with a suitcase. Without a word he opened it and took some things out. He set a cap on the porch step and put a quarter in it. Next thing you know, a wooden puppet was dancing back and forth between the bars, and then it was dancing on the steps. It had a red cap and whiskers and a harp under one arm. Another one came out and danced, too, and they sang a song in another language—Italian, I guess. Everybody watched and smiled. We knew he'd brought those puppets over on the boat with him. And he hadn't shown them to us for all those years.

Right near the end of the show I looked around. Who should be right behind me but Miss Marlow? I knew Maxine had sent her a note about the fair, but I hadn't really thought she'd come. She saw me and smiled. I smiled back. I was on cloud nine. I yelled over to Ben, "Sell those last pieces of cake for a quarter apiece," just to let her know I was in charge. A minute later I felt her hand on my arm. "This is so nice, Vernon," she said. "I'm sure it means a great deal to Ronald."

"Yes, ma'am." I felt like I'd swallowed my own tongue.

"I'll see you later," she said.

I thought she'd left when it happened, but I wasn't sure. There was so much going on that I didn't notice the commotion until Sandra came and got me.

"Vern!" she shouted. "She's drunk!"

"Where?"

"This way!"

I heard her before I saw her. "Get out of my way, you goddamn busybody!" she was screaming. "Let me alone!"

Someone answered, but I couldn't hear what they said.

"Don't touch Ronald!" she screamed.

The crowd made way for me. She was standing in front of Etta's pie table, waving an empty bottle of Southern Comfort over her head. Etta and Mrs. Moore were trying to calm her down. Ronald was cringing behind her. Then she saw me. "Ronald and I don't need anybody's charity!" she hollered.

"He's just trying to do you a good turn, Maxine," Etta said. "You ought to be grateful to the boy."

"I ain't grateful to nobody!"

"Shame on you. And look at poor Ronald. You've got him all shook up."

"Don't say nothing about Ronald. He's my son! Nobody can talk about Ronald but me!"

"You and your foolishness," Mrs. Moore said. "Go on home and have some coffee."

"Shut up, you old busybody!"

Maxine grabbed Ronald by the arm. She jerked him away from us, toward her house. "Good-bye and go to hell!" she shouted. The last we saw of her, she was weaving down her own block, with Ronald behind her.

14

I WAS SO MAD, I CUSSED HER the whole time we carried tables back to the church. "I'm through with her," I told Jerry. "She's a basket case."

Etta's brother overheard me. "Don't let her get on your nerves," he said. "She'll be at your door tomorrow as meek as a kitten. She knows Ronald needs shoes. And with what you raised today, she'll be able to buy him more than that."

I counted the money after supper. I did it twice, just to be sure. We earned $143 for Ronald. The stack of bills was as thick as my arm, and the change filled two canning jars.

"You need a truck just to get it to the bank," Daddy said. He smiled at me shyly, like I was somebody he'd never met. And for a minute I thought maybe I was.

After all, I'd thought up the fair, organized it, and made sure it went smoothly. It had been almost perfect.

"If only Maxine hadn't gotten drunk . . ."

Tony was sitting with his back to us. "You should have realized she'd do something," he said matter-of-factly. "She couldn't stand for someone else to be the star of the show, even if it was Ronald."

He was right, I saw suddenly, but I felt the blood run to my head. "Why didn't you say that before the fair, so I could do something about it?"

He shrugged. "It was your show, Vern."

"And if I screwed it up, all the better for you. I'd still be dumb Vernon, your stupid little brother!" The words came out hard as bullets, but they weren't enough. I grabbed Tony by the collar. His eyes rolled back.

"I never said that."

"But it's what you thought!"

"Get off me!"

"Vernon!" Daddy's hand was on my shoulder, pulling me back, but I ignored him.

"You didn't think I could do it, did you? And you didn't want me to, either, because for once, I'd have done something as well as you!"

"Get off me!"

"It's true, isn't it? It's true!" I let him go.

"Goddamnit," Tony said, rubbing his neck. His eyes filled up and mine did, too. I pushed past Ben and Sandra, who were standing in the door with their mouths open. I went up the stairs four at a time and slammed the door of my room behind me. I threw myself on the bed and let it all hang out.

When I woke up, I was sprawled on the bedspread with my clothes still on. My mouth tasted like dirt. It was morning. If he'd slept in the other bed, Tony had already left for school. I was glad he was gone.

Some people say that hollering can get a load off your chest, but it didn't work that way for me. Instead of feeling better, I felt madder. It was like I'd discovered a splinter buried under my skin, and that yelling had been the first couple of yanks, trying to get it out. But it was still in there, needling me. The only way I could forget about it was to leave the house, and then it was only a little better, because even on the street nobody left me alone. "The fair was a lot of fun," they called out. "How much money did you make for Ronald?" The little kids tagged around after me like I had candy in my pockets.

"I'm sorry I missed it," Miss Annie said the next day. "I can't make it more than half a block on this darn walker. But the neighbors told me it was wonderful."

"Did you hear Maxine got drunk?"

She nodded. "It's a shame, but there's not a thing you could have done to stop her."

"Tony would have thought of something. He figured

83

out she'd screw up because she wanted all the attention."

"Tony." Miss Annie frowned. "He's the thin, blond one, the one who's always by himself?" I thought she was thinking of someone else, but she went on: "He's usually got an armload of books, doesn't he?"

"That's right."

"So *he* would have thought of something." She let the words roll off her tongue, as if she were enjoying the idea of Tony and Maxine face-to-face. To me it wasn't funny.

"He's smart."

"So am I, and I've never been able to control Maxine. The only one who can control her is Ronald."

"Ronald!" For a minute I thought she was kidding. Then I remembered Maxine describing the days after he was born. "She got a job, to prove she could take care of him." I nodded.

"Yes, and she kept it for twelve years. Even now Maxine usually has Ronald ready for the bus, and is there to pick him up after school."

"He has to listen to her holler, though."

Miss Annie sighed. "That's the least of what he has to put up with, I'm afraid. The winter before last Maxine dragged him around in weather so cold, he ended up with frostbite in three toes. And that April—just about a year ago, in fact—she passed out at the bus station downtown. The police found Ronald wandering around by himself. They tried to get him into foster care, but

84

the judge ruled in her favor."

"They couldn't take Ronald away. He's her son."

"They could, too. Once you're down and out, anything can happen." Miss Annie stared at me like she could read the question in my mind. "It's different for the two of us," she said quietly. "We're"—she paused, searching for the right word—"connected."

"What do you mean?"

"We're on track with the rest of the city. We go to bed at night and get up in the morning, and most days we have plans, whether we like them or not. We have breakfast before and supper afterward. And if we don't show up or answer the phone for a day, someone will notice."

"You check on Maxine, and Mrs. Moore does, too."

"We try. But I can't get around well, and Clarice has a job. If Maxine disappears, it could be a few days before we know." Miss Annie looked out the window. I did, too, half expecting to see Maxine and Ronald on the sidewalk. But there was only a dirty sheet of newspaper, tumbling over and over in the wind.

"I wonder where they are now."

"I saw the bus pull up a while ago, so Ronald must be home. More than likely they're both in there, watching Mickey Mouse." Miss Annie smiled. She reached over to the little carved desk near the sofa and picked something up. "I meant to give you this when you first came in," she said. "It's a present."

"For me?"

She nodded and handed me—

"A book . . ." I couldn't hide my disappointment, and after the disappointment came anger. For a few minutes I'd forgotten about Tony and his straight-A brain. "You know I'm no good at reading," I said crossly.

"But you're getting better. And this is one of my favorite books. I read it to all my classes."

I looked at the picture on the cover. There were a boy and girl about Sandra's age, with a gray mutt in between them. I couldn't pronounce the title: *Henry & Beezus.*

"A book can be a friend," Miss Annie said. "When I feel lonely, I slide my chair right over to that big bookcase"—she gestured—"and put out my hand. Whatever it falls on, I pick up and read. By now I know some of those books so well, I think they must know me, too. So we have tea together—Madame Bovary and I. Once I even had tea with Robinson Crusoe."

"Robinson Crusoe's imaginary."

She didn't seem to notice I was irritated. "Not to me," she said brightly.

"To everyone else he is."

"How do you know?"

"Because he's not alive."

"He's alive in my mind, and lots of other people's, too."

I could feel myself getting frustrated. "Miss Annie?"

"Yes?"

"Remember when we were talking about Maxine?

And you said the rest of us are connected to reality?"

She smiled. "I don't believe I used that particular expression," she said.

"The truth is you had tea with yourself."

She crossed her bony arms. "Prove it."

I rolled up the book and stuck it in my pocket. It made an unfamiliar bulge against my side. "Miss Annie," I said, "you're *almost* as crazy as Maxine."

She smiled again. "Lots of people are," she said.

15

MAXINE FOUND ME the next day.

I was standing on the sidewalk outside Milt's, digging the last crumbs out of a bag of cheese curls, when she came by. At first she acted like she was on her way somewhere else. I ignored her. I crumpled the bag into a ball and tossed it into the air, then turned like I was about to leave.

"Vernon?" She came across the street fast. She was wearing red plastic snow boots—the kind kids wear, with elastic bands at the top—and a plastic rain bonnet. I looked up into the sky. It was clear blue.

"Where you been?" Maxine said. "You haven't come down to see us."

"I been around."

"What you been up to?"

"Nothing much." I tossed the bag up in the air,

caught it again. "Had a busy weekend, though."

"Annie said you made a lot of money for Ronald."

"A hundred and forty-three dollars." I said it casual, like it was nothing.

"Bless you, Vernon."

I didn't say anything. I wondered if she was going to ask for it, after what she'd said about not needing charity. But she grabbed my sleeve. "I'm sorry," she said. "I was so excited, I took a drink to calm my nerves. I never meant to leave the house. I hope Ronald's teacher wasn't there."

"I think she'd left."

"I hope so. Once I get around people, I just can't stop myself."

"I was mad as hell." I was surprised when the words came out. I wondered if I was going to tell her about how I'd yelled at Tony; and then, quick, like it didn't really matter, I did. Her blue eyes fastened right on me. When I finished, she sighed and shifted her striped pocketbook from one arm to the other.

"I can't believe anyone would think you're dumb, Vernon," she said. "All the things you've done for us. And Ronald likes you more than anybody."

"Just 'cause Ronald likes me doesn't make me smart."

"It does, too. Ronald *knows*." She nodded her head like I'd asked a question, and she was answering. "He can't talk, but he knows who's smart. And he knows some people look down on him. Those are the dumb ones."

"Liking Ronald doesn't have anything to do with doing good in school."

"Doing good in school doesn't have anything to do with being smart, either! Look at me! I only went through tenth grade!"

I looked at Maxine, with her rain bonnet, boots, and rainbow-striped pocketbook, and the laughs began to bubble up in me like bubbles in a fish tank. There was nothing I could do to stop myself. But she thought it was funny, too, or else maybe she thought *I* was funny. So we both stood there cracking up.

It took me a while to catch my breath. "You're nuts!" I said. But she only laughed harder.

"Ronald knows!" she said.

"Knows what?" A crowd of kids had gathered behind us. I guess they were wondering what could be so funny.

"None of your beeswax," Maxine said. "Now get out of here, before I sic King Kong on you."

"You don't know King Kong."

"She does too!" a boy hollered. "She keeps him locked in her basement!"

"Crazy lady!"

I made a grab for one of them and they scattered. We looked at each other and laughed again.

I arranged to take Ronald shopping on Saturday at ten o'clock. I asked Bobby and Jerry and Chris if they wanted to go, but they looked at me like *I* was nuts. I guess it was one thing to raise money for Ronald and another to walk down the street beside him.

I didn't tell Daddy or the other kids about it. At home I still felt bruised, as if that old splinter had made my skin raw all over. It wasn't just Tony—there was nothing any of them could say that didn't irritate me. Not only that, but the more they tried to build me up, the madder I felt. It was as if the fair had finally proved that I was capable, and all my years of wondering was their fault.

16

I KNOCKED BUT NO ONE CAME to the door except Brownie. Yap! Yap! Yap!

"Shut up!" somebody yelled. I pushed the door open and went in.

"He's almost ready." Maxine was holding a bar of soap in one hand and a comb in the other. She had Ronald in a kitchen chair. He looked at me like he was a prisoner of war and I was his savior. "Hold still!" Maxine fussed. She washed his ears and then combed his hair. "Isn't he handsome, Vern?"

I nodded.

"All done," she said. Ronald struggled to his feet.

I wondered if he'd be afraid to leave her, but he wasn't. He only looked back once. She was standing beside the hedge, watching us, and when he looked back, she waved.

"We're going up Filmore to Preston, and from there to the top of the hill where the highway is," I explained. "The Army-Navy store is in the first block, and the shoe store is across the street. And if we have money left over, we'll get some ice cream. You like ice cream, don't you?"

Ronald nodded. He reached toward my coat pocket.

"Not now—later, when we're done shopping. Anyway, I can't keep ice cream in my pocket, because it melts. Do you know what that means?"

He looked at me with a question in his eyes.

"It means it gets soft and starts dripping. And if it melts all the way, it drips into a puddle, like water. It's not good to eat that way. It would mess up my pocket, too."

We went on. We saw some people we knew, and they waved and spoke: "This is the big day, huh, Vern? Have a good time!"

A couple little kids tagged behind us. "Can we go? Pul-leeze? We want to see what he gets!"

"I can tell you what you're going to get if you don't get out of here!"

"No fair!"

But they did leave, scooting back across the road to play catch or hopscotch on the sidewalk till the grownups told them to move on. Ronald watched them for a moment. They made him nervous, I could tell, and I think they made him sad, too. I wondered if he wished he could be one of them.

I thought of the things he loved, and listed them out loud to make him feel better: "*Lassie*, spaghetti, soda, biscuits, Brownie," and then the people: "Maxine, Miss Marlow, Miss Annie." I even included myself. He stopped and stared. I guess it was like hearing all the good news at once. I laughed. And then we were there.

"Pants and shirts, first, then shoes." I opened the door of the Army-Navy store. The fat guy behind the counter frowned at us, but I kept my cool, remembering the wad of bills in my pocket. "My friend needs three pairs of pants and three flannel shirts," I said, handing him a list of sizes Maxine had given me.

"I've seen that kid before," the guy said, not sounding mean so much as curious. "Ain't he out on the street with his old lady sometimes?"

"Could be."

"Ain't she kind of a nut?"

I didn't say anything, but I guess he thought I agreed.

"It's pitiful how she treats the kid, dragging him around in the rain and snow. I guess social services caught up with her. That where you're from?"

"No."

He looked at me again. "Why, you're only a kid yourself," he said.

The pants and shirts were nice, folded and with that new smell that goes away when you wash them. I let Ronald pick the shirt patterns. He picked everything blue: blue-and-green plaid, blue-and-navy plaid, blue and red checks. Then we got him socks, T-shirts and underwear. The bill came to $92.00. I counted out a hundred while the guy stared. Then I figured it out in my head, 100–92=8, and that's how much he gave me back, a five and three ones. "Come back," he said.

"Sure thing."

Shoe City is in what used to be the Tenley Heights Theater, except that on the marquee where they used to advertise movies, now they spell out the latest style of tennis shoes, and what a bargain they're supposed to be: Nikes $41, or Reeboks $39.99. There's always a crowd around the window, wishing they had money. So I didn't pay any attention until somebody said, "Hey, Vern." Bobby and Jerry and Chris were standing there.

"We decided we couldn't leave an important decision like Ronald's shoes up to you. I mean, you been wearing cowboy boots all spring."

I grinned. They always give me a hard time about my boots.

"We been waiting forever," Bobby said. "Come on, let's go in."

We had a terrible time deciding what to get. Jerry thought Adidas, and Chris was inclined to a pair of Nikes that were too much money. Ronald didn't know what he wanted—he'd point at this pair, but as soon as

95

the next box got opened he wanted that one, too. The salesman was real nice about it. He kept the shoes coming: black ones and white ones and everything in between. It was Bobby who found them, though, and when he did everyone—especially Ronald—knew they were right. They were Converse, with red-and-white checks and red laces. As soon as Ronald had them on, we hollered, "Right on, man! Give me five!" Ronald was smiling from ear to ear.

He wore them home. We bought ice cream at the deli and walked down the hill together, right in the middle of the street. When we got to my block, who should be standing on the corner but Maxine herself. Ronald stopped dead. He held up one foot and then the other.

"Would you look at that!" Maxine said. "Checkerboard shoes!"

"They're Converse!" a little kid yelled. "Ronald has Converse!"

"What's Converse?" Mr. Frank heard the commotion and leaned out from his porch.

"It's them kind of high tops," Mrs. Harris said. She would know, too. Her son Gary has a closetful of tennis shoes.

"Looks like he likes them. Look at him smile!"

Near the end of the block Mitchell's little sister Keesha ran up and stopped right in front of Ronald. She stared at his feet. "I want some," she said. I don't know who she was talking to, but Maxine must have thought it was her.

"Ask Santa, or the tooth fairy!" she said. "Or call President Reagan. Tell him you live in Tenley Heights, and you want some shoes like Ronald's."

Keesha giggled. "I don't think he buys shoes for kids."

"You never know until you try."

Keesha shrugged. Her big brown eyes rested on Ronald's face for just a moment. "You got new shoes," she told him. He nodded.

"He knows he got new shoes!" Maxine shouted. "He's got new everything!" She pointed at the shopping bag I was holding and smiled at me. I noticed she was wearing purple lipstick.

"You're our best friend, Vernon," she said in front of everyone. "Thanks."

17

I WENT DOWN TO MISS ANNIE'S after church. I pretended I had a question about my homework, but the truth was I felt bad that I hadn't thanked her for the present. She didn't seem to mind, though. And she'd seen Ronald's shoes.

"They came over yesterday to watch a movie with me," she explained. "*Othello*, with Paul Robeson. Have you heard of him?"

"Can't say that I have, or the movie either."

"It's based on a play by Shakespeare."

The idea of Maxine and Ronald watching a Shakespeare play struck me funny. "Did they enjoy it?" I asked.

"Not as much as I did," Miss Annie admitted. "Ronald could hardly take his eyes off his new shoes, and Maxine wanted a beer to go with the popcorn I made. The language got on her nerves, too."

"She's the last one who should be fussing about bad language. Why, she taught *me* a thing or two when we first met."

Miss Annie laughed. "It wasn't cursing that bothered her, Vernon. Shakespearian English can be hard to understand."

"Is it worse than regular English?"

"It's different. It's lovely, actually."

"Oh." I made a mental note to skip tenth-grade English if there was any way possible. Steph had told me they read *Romeo and Juliet*.

"I could recite a speech from *Othello*, if you'd like. . . ." Miss Annie was on a roll. "There are all sorts of good ones."

"That's okay . . . I told Daddy I'd be home soon."

She called me back before I could escape. "Vernon?"

"Yes ma'am?"

"There's something I'd like you to do one afternoon this week. Something for Maxine."

"What?"

"I'd like you to dig her a garden. I've ordered some seeds through the mail, so she won't have to pay for them. The vegetables will be good for Ronald. And there's nothing nicer than seeing flowers out the window." She pulled the curtain back, as if they were already there.

"A garden has to be taken care of, doesn't it? Watered and all?"

"That's true." Miss Annie nodded. "But Maxine might do that."

Or I might do it, because you'll make me, I thought. But I didn't complain.

"Where do you want it?"

"Right there, in between her house and mine." She was still holding the curtain back when I saw something that surprised me. "That's Miss Marlow!" I said. "She's sitting in her car outside Maxine's house!"

"Miss Marlow?"

"Ronald's teacher. She's nice, and she's good-looking too. I'm going to say hi."

But by the time I got to the sidewalk, Miss Marlow was pulling away. I meant to ask Maxine about it, but I'd told the guys I'd watch basketball with them. So I headed over to Bobby's, whistling to myself.

We had a real nice evening. Bobby's mom had made carrot cake just for us. The game was close, but our team won. Afterward I told the guys about seeing Miss Marlow's car.

"Somebody as beautiful as she is doesn't need to be nice, too," I said. "But she is."

"She's a looker," Bobby said. "I saw her at the fair. If I had a teacher like her, I'd go to class every day."

I walked home dreaming about her. Though I'd only met her twice, I thought I knew her through and through.

18

I DON'T MIND DIGGING THAT MUCH, to tell you the truth. There's a smell that comes with the dirt in spring, a kind of thawing, rotting smell, that I happen to like. I like the smell of hot tar, too, which makes Steph hold her nose. I told that to Maxine while we were digging in the yard, her and Ronald and me. "That's 'cause you're a city boy," she said. "Only a city boy could like the smell of tar."

"I couldn't live out in the sticks. Heck, I've heard they don't even have sidewalks there."

But she wasn't in a joking mood. "I never saw a sidewalk till I left North Carolina. Once I got here, I never wanted to go back. I liked the hustle and bustle and the parties, and I liked dressing up and walking downtown, knowing everyone was watching me."

"Ronald's a city boy like me, aren't you, Ronald?

Here, have a piece of gum." I gave it to him quick, before Maxine could intercept it.

"You know that's bad for his teeth, Vernon!"

"He'll survive."

"That's easy for you to say! You aren't responsible for him."

"Touchy, aren't you?"

"Maybe I have good reason."

Ronald whined. He hated it when we bickered.

"Miss Marlow dropped by Sunday," Maxine said out of the blue. "She said she happened to be passing by."

"I know! I saw her car out the window when I was at Miss Annie's. I came out fast, but she pulled away before I got the chance to talk to her." I bent over and mashed a clod of dirt. "She must really like Ronald."

"I guess." Maxine seemed distracted.

"She's pretty, too."

"Pretty! If you had to fill out all the damn forms she sends home, you wouldn't be thinking about pretty!"

"My dad has to sign forms for five kids, so he taught us to fill them out ourselves." I didn't want Maxine to know he couldn't read and write. "It's no big deal."

"It is to me. I don't like other people nosing around in Ronald's and my business. When did he get his shots? What does he eat for dinner? When's his bedtime?" She frowned. "I feel like they're looking over my shoulder," she said. "Next they'll want to know what color toilet paper we buy."

That cracked me up. "What color *do* you buy?" I asked, trying to keep a straight face.

But she didn't think it was funny. "Shut up, Vernon," she snapped. She hardly laughed again for the rest of the afternoon.

Her mood was contagious. Ronald whined for more gum, pulling on my pocket and stamping his feet when I said no. He shifted from side to side, clutching the old gum wrapper in both hands. Finally he made me nervous, too. "Leave me alone, would you? I've got all this left to dig, and the dirt's got to be broken up, to boot. At this rate we'll be here till midnight." I turned my back on him.

He surprised us, though. Maxine went into the house for coffee and came back with three cups balanced on a plate. I put the shovel down and took a drink. That was when I noticed. "He's working," I told Maxine. "Look!"

Ronald had the hoe in both hands, and he was chopping to beat the band. Dirt was flying.

"Did you show him how to do that?"

She shook her head. "I told you he knows more than he lets on."

"Ronald, take a break! Have some coffee."

He ignored me.

"I didn't mean to hurt your feelings."

Ronald looked up. I could see he was still mad.

"I'm *sorry*!"

He stopped then, but only for a minute. Then it was

back to work: *whap! whap! whap!*

"He must have Carolina in his blood," Maxine murmured.

But I shook my head. "He's a city boy, like me."

19

JERRY CLUED ME IN THAT something might be wrong. "Guess what happened last night?" he said. "Miss Marlow called!"

"She did?"

He nodded. "She and Dad talked at the fair, and Dad told her about John. She volunteered to send information about a program that might be good for him. She called to get our address, but after that she asked questions about Maxine and Ronald."

"What kind of questions?"

"Like how long they'd been in the neighborhood, and how well we knew them. She asked about Ronald's father, too, and whether he took care of Ronald when Maxine got drunk."

"You mean she knows Maxine's an alcoholic?"

"She must. I guess someone told her. Or else she saw her at the fair."

"She'd gone home before Maxine came," I said quickly. "I'm sure she had."

"It doesn't matter *how* she found out." Jerry's voice was calm. "What matters is that she did."

"But if she didn't *see* her, it's not important. People gossip, you know, Jerr? They could say anything."

"Like what?"

"Like that she's crazy, or she drinks. . . ."

Jerry looked at me funny. "That's not gossip. It's the truth."

For a minute I didn't answer. It's strange: Of all the names kids call you, one thing I'd never been called was a liar. Sandra was the one who made stuff up: even little things, like what she had for lunch, or who sat by her on the bus. The few times I tried fibbing I got caught right away, and in the long run I decided not lying was easier. But now I wasn't so sure. I thought about it for a while. "It's part of the truth," I said slowly. "But there's more to it than that. And if Miss Marlow found out someone's crazy, or a drunk, she might not take the time to see what else they are too."

"What do you mean?"

"Maxine's a good mother, mostly."

Jerry didn't say anything.

"She is. You just have to know her, that's all."

"Maybe you should tell that to Miss Marlow."

Jerry sounded doubtful, but I realized suddenly that it wasn't a bad idea.

"Maybe I will," I said. "Maybe I'll write her a letter."

"What will you say, Vern? She's not as crazy as she acts, and she only gets loaded once a week?"

"She doesn't get loaded once a week."

"Maybe not since you've known her. But Mom says she used to get looped for a month at a time. And Ronald had to tag along behind her."

"I don't believe that!"

He shrugged.

"I don't!"

We ended up okay. I remembered I'd told him he could have my baseball card collection, and I ran in the house and got it. He sat on the curb leafing through the cards, which I kept in a couple of shoe boxes. "This Cal Ripken could be worth a lot of money," he told me. "You sure you want to give it up?"

"You can have it.

"And Camillo Pasqual—that one's got some age on it. Did you trade for it?"

"Naw, it was probably Tony's."

"Man, with these added to mine, I'm going to have the whole 'sixty-eight Pirates squad. The whole squad. I can't believe it. Thanks, Vern."

"That's all right."

"See you later." He stuck the shoe boxes under his arm. "Hope it works out with Miss Marlow."

"I expect it will."

He went on down the street.

I wrote the letter that night. I used notebook paper and looked up the words I wasn't sure about.

> *Dear Miss Marlow,*
>
> *I just want to tell you that no matter what you saw at the fair, Maxine is a good mother. She cares about Ronald a great deal. When problems come up, the neighbors help with him, and I do, too.*
>
> *If you have any questions about the situation, please call me, Vernon Dibbs. My phone number is 555-1098.*
>
> *Yours truly,*
> *Vernon Dibbs*
> *P.S. We will see you at the Special Olympics!*

I read the letter over three times, then folded it and stuck it in an envelope. I sat there holding it awhile. Should I tell Maxine what Jerry'd said, and what I'd done? She would be mad, I knew; the last thing she wanted was one more person sticking their nose in her business. But I'd thought the fair up in the first place, and run it, too. If Miss Marlow had seen Maxine there, I was responsible.

I wouldn't tell Maxine, I decided. She didn't need another worry. I wrote Miss Marlow's name on the envelope and looked up the address of Ronald's school in the phone book. I stamped the letter and stuffed it in the mailbox on the corner.

20

DADDY TALKED TO ME ABOUT the fight. He waited for a night when Tony and Steph had gone out and the little kids were in bed. I didn't want to talk about it, and when he came into the room, I got my jacket like I had something else to do.

"Where you headed, Son?"

"Over Jerry's."

"You boys ever get that ten-speed fixed?"

"Not yet."

He shook his head. "They make them things so complicated—the old bikes we could tear down and put back together in an hour. We kids used to do that for fun, out in the alley, tires and chains and axles lying everywhere." He stopped. "Before you go, Vern . . ."

"Yeah?"

"I want to say something about the other night."

"What night?"

He looked at me sadly. I guess he could see I wasn't going to help him out. "The night you hollered at Tony."

"What about it?"

"You shouldn't have grabbed his neck. He had a great big welt there the next day." Daddy coughed. I kept quiet, hoping it was over.

"People go up and down this street with all kinds of bruises, and I know they got drunk or mad and beat up on each other—you've heard them Saturday nights, just like I have. But I always told myself we were different. We might get mad, but we'd settle our arguments without fighting." He looked at me. I turned red.

"Tony thinks he's . . ." I started, but Daddy shook his head.

"I know all that, and I know why you did it," he said quietly. "And I'm not saying what you think is wrong. I'm saying you can't fight him."

I just stood there.

"You're a big boy, Vern. You could hurt somebody."

"They all pick on me." I knew it sounded childish, and I hated it as soon as it came out.

"We have our problems." Daddy sounded tired. "And I'm thinking about them."

Thinking doesn't help, a voice inside me said. But I kept quiet, and he told me I could go.

On Sunday Maxine invited me down for macaroni

and cheese. That morning she laughed when I saw her on the street, and when she came to the door, she was smiling too. Ronald was on the couch watching TV. His Converse were on the kitchen table.

"He's driving me nuts!" Maxine said. "He wants to wear those damn shoes every minute! And if I don't let him, they have to be right where he can see them, so he knows they're still here."

"Why don't you let him?"

"I'm afraid they'll get worn out before the Olympics. Ronald can be hard on shoes."

"Those Converse are high quality."

"So are Ronald's feet, and they come down hard on whatever's under them. He weighs near a hundred and thirty-five pounds."

"That's not much. I weigh a hundred and sixty myself, and I'm younger than Ronald; shorter, too."

"You're on the chunky side, all right."

"You make it sound like I'm fat."

"I didn't say that."

But she didn't say I wasn't, either. I gave her a dirty look and went to sit with Ronald. He checked my pocket for treats. Then he pointed to the TV. A preacher was talking to a woman in a wheelchair. "Give your heart to Him, that you may walk!" he shouted. Ronald tugged at my sleeve. He wanted to know what was going on.

"He's going to ask us to pray, so she'll be saved," I told him. "Only it's just an act. They do it so people will send them money."

Sure enough, the preacher put his hand on the woman's head. He and the audience said a bunch of prayers. Then the woman got out of the wheelchair and walked around the stage. The audience clapped. Ronald clapped too.

"I told you, you can't believe everything you see, Ronald." He ignored me. He pointed to a girl on crutches. Now the preacher started in on her.

"What's your name, honey?"

"Roberta."

"How old are you?"

"Six."

"How long have you been crippled?"

"All my life."

"Let me touch your head, and we'll pray together." There was a silence. Then the girl threw the crutches into the air. She jumped up and hugged a woman on the other side of the stage. The audience went crazy. Ronald clapped too.

"I'll pray for you at home," the preacher said. The camera panned in till his face looked big. Ronald leaned forward so his nose was about a foot from the screen. I put my hand on his shoulder.

"Ronald, this is a bunch of mumbo-jumbo. You should change the channel before you get worked up over nothing."

"Huh!" I hadn't noticed Maxine behind me. She must have been watching too. "Catholics believe more

112

mumbo-jumbo than anybody," she said. "They use necklaces to say their prayers."

"Those aren't necklaces, they're rosaries!"

"Rosary, schmozarie." She made a face.

"My mother used to say the rosary every night." I felt my scalp getting hot.

"Well, if she said it, it must be right!"

"You take that back!"

"I won't! You're such a goody-goody, Vernon! You think if your mother—"

Wham! We turned in time to see Ronald's foot bounce off the TV. He folded his arms across his chest and started screeching. His face was bright red.

"He's having a tantrum. Stop it, Ronald! What if Miss Marlow came by now, like she did on Friday?" Maxine sat down by him. "Vernon and I don't have to agree on everything just to make you happy. Now stop."

Ronald carried on for another minute or two. Then he got interested in a commercial. Maxine went back to the kitchen. She was wearing slippers and a faded housecoat. "Vernon, you set the table, and I'll heat some bread. There's a jug of pop in the refrigerator."

"Okay." I was so glad we'd stopped arguing that I didn't ask about Miss Marlow. But I was nervous as I put down the silverware and cups. Ronald noticed that, I think. He got up from the couch and showed me his Converse.

"Beautiful! The colors are perfect for you! And it won't be long before you get to wear them."

"When is it, anyway?"

"June fifteenth."

"Five weeks," Maxine said to herself. She'd washed off her makeup, and her face looked pale and puffy.

"It'll be here in no time," I told Ronald.

21

SANDRA FOUND THE BOOK, which meant she'd
been looking through my coat pockets. I didn't figure
that part out till later, though. I'd come home early because the electricity went out at school. The elementary schools get out at noon on Wednesdays, too,
because they have teachers' meetings in the afternoons.
Usually Sandra and Ben check in with Mrs. Murphy
next door and then hang out in front of the TV. They
weren't expecting me.

I wouldn't have noticed anything if she hadn't
winced when I came in. "What's that?"

"Nothing."

She'd stuck something under her sweatshirt. As flat as
she is, I knew it wasn't part of her. I grabbed her arm.
"Get off," she said, hitting at me. The something fell.
It was a book—a dirty one, I figured. I was surprised

when I turned it over.

"That's mine! Miss Annie gave it to me."

She didn't say anything at first. Then she whined, "I only want to read it."

"You have to ask before you take my stuff."

"I'm asking."

"But you took it first. Not only that, but you went in my room to find it."

"Did not!"

"Then where'd you get it?"

"I found it on the sidewalk."

"Liar!" I grabbed it and headed upstairs. She was blubbering in the living room. But partway up the stairs I overheard Ben say, "Remember when Mom used to take us to the library?" That made me stop and think.

The library used to be open late on Tuesdays, and we'd all go, all but Daddy. Mom would sit with me and Sandra and Ben in the kids' section. We'd take down a stack of books and fuss and argue until we'd picked the six we could check out. Then we'd go home together.

Walking home in the dark with that stack of books was a great feeling. I knew Mom would read me a new story every night for six days. But nobody read to Ben and Sandra—not now. They had to take care of themselves.

Why hadn't I thought about that before? I stood in the stairwell awhile longer. Then I turned and went back down. Sandra was on the couch, holding her Barbie. Her eyes were red.

"You can borrow the book," I said gruffly. "I'm sorry I yanked it away."

"I can?" She dropped the Barbie and grabbed the book as if she was afraid I'd change my mind.

"Yeah. It was too babyish for me anyway."

"Ben! Vernon said I can borrow it!" He came in from the kitchen, looking surprised. "I'll read some to you," she said. "Sit right here, so you can see the pictures."

They sat together for a half hour while I was in the kitchen doing my grammar exercises. I'd hear Sandra's voice going along smooth till she got to a word she didn't know. Sometimes she'd sound it out, but other times she'd just have to skip it. Once I heard her puzzling over something and realized it was the word "deliver"—I could tell from the rest of the sentence, which was about Henry being a paper boy. So I yelled it in there, and she said, "Oh, that's it!" I felt pretty good, you know? And it turned out the story wasn't so stupid after all. Henry and this girl Beezus got into all kinds of scrapes with their neighbor, who didn't like kids. It reminded me of stuff Jerry and Bobby and I used to do.

Sandra told Daddy about it that night: "Vern let me read his book! I read thirty-five pages without making a single mistake!"

"I didn't know Vern had a book," Tony said.

I started to say something mean back, but Sandra beat me to it. "He does, too! Miss Annie gave it to him. Right, Vern?"

I nodded.

"I never see her anymore," Steph said. "She used to walk past every day. She had such a nice smile."

"Her arthritis got so bad, she hardly goes out."

"Poor thing. I guess she's shut up all alone."

"No, she isn't," Ben said. "Vern goes down there, and so does Mrs. Moore, and Maxine and Ronald. And Mitchell and I went to see her yesterday. She knew our names, and she gave us candy."

"Why'd you go to see her?"

"We seen a stray cat under her porch, and we wanted to know could we have it. It was black with a white spot on its tail."

"I hope she said no," Daddy said.

"She didn't say yes or no. She said it's named Frederick Douglass and it lives under there, and she'd ask it the next time she saw it whether it wanted a boy like me for a pet." Ben frowned. His round face was grubby. "Do you think it'll want me?"

"Not unless you take a bath."

"Do I have to?"

"Let's vote on it." Daddy winked.

"Yes!" we shouted.

Then Ben noticed he was in the spotlight. He put his fingers in his ears, stuck out his tongue, and giggled like crazy.

22

"**T**HE SEEDS CAME!"

Miss Annie was smiling, and the sun was shining through her front window like it was going to sprout us instead of lettuces and sunflowers. I put my homework on the coffee table. She gave me some parts of speech to sort out and then corrected the papers I'd brought. She was moving fast. I could tell she intended to get me out in that garden today.

"This is excellent, Vernon. You even got *winning* where I used it as a noun. That use of a participle is called a gerund." She spelled it, but I could tell her heart was outside. "I'll give you some more tomorrow. But now—"

"You'd like me to help Maxine and Ronald plant the garden."

"Vernon, you're a mind reader! Would you?"

119

"Yeah, only . . ."

"What?"

"Maxine's been in an awful mood lately," I blurted. "Every time I'm around her, we end up in a fight."

"You won't this afternoon, because she isn't home. She and Ronald had to keep an appointment downtown." Miss Annie frowned. "She did seem glum. I wonder if there's a problem."

I was scared to tell her, but I did. "Miss Marlow knows Maxine's an alcoholic, and she called Jerry's dad asking questions. And she's been dropping by Maxine's house, too. I'm afraid she'll go there when Maxine's drunk."

"Goodness, Vernon—slow down." Miss Annie sounded grave. "How long have you known about this?"

"A week or two. Jerry told me about the phone call."

"You should have told me."

"I didn't want to, because it's my fault."

"Because you managed the fair?"

I nodded miserably.

"Nonsense. Maxine is an adult, and she's responsible for her own behavior. You have to understand that." She stared at me until I nodded again. Then she said, "Bring me the telephone."

She dialed a couple of numbers without looking them up. She left a message at the first one, but the other was answered by someone she called Sam. She asked me to step outside so she could speak to him in private. "In fact, you can get the hoe off the back porch

120

and start in the garden. I'll let you know when I'm off the phone."

It was lonely out there. I wondered who Sam was and what he knew. Once I looked in and saw Miss Annie gesturing with one hand as if she were angry. Finally her head appeared at the window. "We'll know more in a few days," she said.

"He couldn't tell you anything?"

"Nothing definite. But don't worry until I tell you to—okay?"

I looked up. She was smiling. An awful weight lifted off my insides—even my arms felt lighter. She propped her elbows on the windowsill, watching me.

"Be sure to read the directions on the seed packets!" she called. "And make the rows the proper distance apart!"

"All right."

"The beets have to be sowed carefully, with a sweeping motion of your arm, and the soil they go into needs to be worked until it's almost as fine as sand."

"Sand! I'll have to hoe all day before this dirt will be as fine as sand!"

"Just ten minutes will make a big difference."

"All right." My left hand felt like it was getting a blister, and my back hurt, too. "Miss Annie?"

"What?"

"This is as fine as I can get it."

"Let me see. Hold some up and drop it."

I did. The dirt splattered off my boot.

"Okay, you can go ahead and plant them."

She didn't let up. Near the end I turned toward the window. "How do you know so much about gardening, anyway?" I asked. "I thought you'd lived in the city all your life."

"Books." She pronounced the word like it was money in the bank.

I groaned out loud. The sweat was pouring off my forehead.

"I got a new name for you, Miss Annie."

"What, Vernon?"

"You're a book-a-holic."

She laughed, and I laughed, too.

23

MAXINE WOULDN'T TELL ME about her appointment. "It's none of your business," she said coldly.

"Why not?"

"'Cause it isn't! Don't be a busybody!"

"I'm not a busybody. I'm just concerned because of something Jerry told me. You see, Miss Marlow—"

"Her again!" Maxine fumed. "I've heard enough about her! Both you and Miss Marlow can butt out!"

"Maxine, I'm trying to tell you something for your own good."

"*I* can decide what's good for me!"

"All right!" I shook my head in disgust. "I give up. But I would like to see Ronald."

"Well, he's busy. You're not his only friend, you know."

"I know he's in there watching TV."

"You know it all, don't you, Vernon?"

I didn't answer. She turned, walked into the house, and slammed the door behind her.

Miss Annie found out what she could. No formal complaint had been made to Protective Services, though they'd received a request for Ronald's records. They wouldn't say who had signed it. "But as long as no complaint is made, there won't be a hearing," Miss Annie said. "And a hearing is the only way a child can be taken from his mother."

"What if they find out Maxine was in jail?"

"I don't know what impact that would have." Miss Annie frowned. I noticed there was a series of wrinkles in her forehead that didn't go away when the frown ended. "I talked to Maxine about it," she said.

"What did she say?"

"She was angry and upset. She said she hadn't had a drink for weeks, and it was getting on her nerves. She never knows when someone might drop by."

"She's nasty to be around. And she's mean to Ronald, too. She wouldn't let me see him yesterday, but I'm going to try again today."

This time she was nicer, and Ronald was glad to see me. We watched *Lassie* together, just like old times, and I taught Brownie to shake hands. Ronald loved that. Every time he did it, Ronald would laugh and laugh.

Later I took Ronald for a walk. He showed me which way he wanted to go, pulling my arm like it was a rudder. We went down Filmore Street and up Montgomery. I tried to turn left at the corner, but Ronald wanted to go straight. He yanked my arm a couple times, then turned and looked at me so hard I had to laugh.

"Come on, dummy," his eyes said.

"Okay, okay," I answered out loud.

He knew where he was going, all right. We stopped in front of a brick rowhouse with a green picket fence. The house was just like every other house on the block, but the yard was full of hokey plaster statues: dogs and squirrels and dwarves and little wheelbarrows and windmills. Right in the middle was a pink crystal ball on a stucco cone. The porch was covered with cat statues: climbing, turning, yowling. There was more junk in that yard than I'd ever laid eyes on.

And Ronald loved it. He stood there with both hands on the fence. His eyes moved from one statue to the next, taking them in slowly. I could tell he wasn't going to leave until he'd stared at every single one.

Then the door opened. A middle-aged woman glared at me. At first I thought she didn't want Ronald there, and I took his arm to move him along, but he shook it free and scowled.

"He isn't done," the woman said. "He's not happy till he's counted them."

"Ronald can't count."

She shrugged. "That's what I thought, too. But his

mother convinced me I was wrong. Watch his lips."

She was so certain, I did. Ronald was on the cats now. Sure enough, every time his gaze shifted, his mouth moved, too. But I couldn't tell what he was murmuring.

"Who are you?" the woman said. I realized her eyes had never left my face.

"Vernon Dibbs. I'm a friend of Ronald's."

"I've never seen him with anyone but Maxine."

"She asked me to take him out because she wasn't feeling good."

"Oh." She eyed me suspiciously. I guess she thought I was a kidnapper. I put on my most innocent face.

"Ready, Ronald?"

He grunted. I saw his lips move again.

"How many are there?" I asked, trying to be polite.

"One hundred and nine," she answered stiffly. She looked at me like I wasn't good enough for Ronald or her.

I practically dragged Ronald out of there. I suppose there were one or two he hadn't looked at yet, and that's why he put up such a fuss. The woman was disapproving. "His mother lets him count them all."

That did it. "Maybe we ought to rename her Saint Maxine," I said nastily.

"You're a very rude boy."

"You ain't heard nothing yet."

"Humph!" She went back in the house with her nose up in the air.

"She's a bitch," I told Ronald on the way home. "And her yard's full of junk." But he was mad at me, too.

I told Maxine the whole story, but by then she was in a lousy mood herself. "Nobody forced you to take him for a walk in the first place," she said.

"He needs his exercise. You-all hardly go out anymore."

"There's nothing to do when you can't drink."

For a minute I thought she was joking, but her eyes looked worn and sad.

24

"**S**TEPH HAS A BOYFRIEND!"

Ben and Mitchell were singsonging on the front porch when I got home from school. I tried to ignore them, but Ben grabbed my leg. "Steph's got a date with Jimmy!" he shouted.

"Who's Jimmy?"

"He's a bagger at the A&P. He asked her yesterday, and they're going to see a movie!"

I went on in the house, feeling grumpy. I'd been looking forward to the big pot of spaghetti Steph usually made on Friday nights. But Steph didn't notice how I felt. She was running around with her hair in curlers.

"What's all this about?"

"Oh, Vern, I'm so glad you're home. I need somebody to go around to Milt's and get me a pair of pantyhose."

"Who's Jimmy? And who's going to make our supper?"

She slowed down and smiled at me. "Did you think I'd fix your supper for the rest of my life?" she asked.

"Daddy can't cook, and neither can Tony or me."

"It's time you learned. I wrote down the recipe, and the ingredients are on the counter."

I plopped myself down on the sofa, still feeling out of sorts. "Who's Jimmy?" I repeated.

"He's that redhead who works with Monica up at the grocery store. He goes to Central—he's on their basketball team, I think."

"They got a lousy team—they hardly won a game."

"Vern!" She flashed me a look.

"Does Daddy know?"

"Yes, and he said I can go. So cheer up, little brother." She tickled me. I can't stand that. I started jumping and laughing at the same time. "Listen," she said when I stopped. "Go get me those pantyhose, size medium in beige."

"Why don't you go?"

"I got curlers in my hair. Come on, Vern."

"I don't have money."

She groaned. "Me, neither."

"How about Tony?"

"I hate to ask him. He's saving for the College Boards, you know." She put her hands on her hips. "I can't go in what I got now, that's for sure. They're full of snags."

"Ask him. All he can say is no."

That's what he said, too; but when she pleaded, he took pity and gave her the money. Daddy made him help make the spaghetti sauce, too. Our problem there was that the recipe didn't say to chop the onion small, or to fry it before you add it to the other stuff. We ate the sauce anyway, except for Ben and Sandra, who asked for plain. Daddy bought some breath mints for the rest of us.

Steph got home late. I heard the car pull up outside, but by then I was half asleep. I wondered if Jimmy kissed her, and if she kissed him back. When I'd seen him at the A&P he'd seemed okay, but not like someone a girl would fall in love with.

It was an okay evening except for something I couldn't get off my mind. It was bad enough to have to ask Milt for a pair of pantyhose, and he knew it. He smirked as he brought them to the register.

"You sure you're a medium, Vern?"

"They're for Steph."

"Beige—is that what you ordered?"

I nodded.

"Total, two ninety-nine." He made a big deal of counting back the penny's worth of change. Then he leaned forward as if he had a secret to tell me.

"Your lady friend was in today," he said.

I didn't have to ask who he meant. "So?"

"I told her I thought she was on the wagon, and

didn't she want to stay that way? And you know what she said?"

"I don't want to know."

But of course he had to tell me: me and everyone else in line.

"Told me to mind my goddamn business," he said. "Can you believe that? She's got a bill as long as history, but she don't mind telling me where to go."

25

I WENT DOWN TO MAXINE'S the next day. I banged on the door but nobody answered. I could hear Brownie barking, and the TV was playing too. "It's me—Vernon," I hollered. "Open up!" But nobody came, and I couldn't tell whether they were home or not.

I kept my eye out for Miss Marlow, and I asked the guys to, too. A couple times I thought I saw her car, but it was already pulling away. Another time I saw it parked on my block. I hung around waiting for her to show up when I should have been doing my homework. Finally two fat guys with briefcases got in the car and slammed the doors. I knocked on the window. One of them rolled it down an inch or two.

"What is it, kid?"

"Isn't this Miss Marlow's Honda?"

"Who's Miss Marlow?"

"She's Ronald's teacher. She's tall, with blond hair . . ."

"Sounds good." The guy rolled the window up and said something to the other one. They both laughed. Then they squealed out of there like I was dirt.

I saw Maxine up on the hill. She wasn't drunk, as far as I could tell, but she did look different. She was wearing a ragged gray coat and trudging along like she had nothing to live for. She didn't know it was me until I said "Hi."

"Vernon!"

"How you doing?"

She looked at me like I was nuts. "How do I look like I'm doing?" she said. Her voice was flat.

"Well, at least you're out of the house."

"I been drunk, but they don't know it yet." She looked around as if Miss Marlow might be spying on us from behind a tree. "I'm close to the end," she said.

"What do you mean? Where's Ronald?"

"Watching *Lassie*. Some things don't change." Just for an instant she smiled, but then her face fell back into a mass of lines.

"They didn't find out, so it's okay. Just don't take another chance!"

"Don't tell me what to do, Vernon," she said tiredly.

"But they could take Ronald!"

"I got it all worked out," she said. "If it comes to that, I mean."

"Worked out how?"

"None of your beeswax." She was getting pissed. By now I knew when to cut my losses.

"I'll see you later," I said.

She turned. "You tried, Vernon," she said. "Nobody can say you didn't try."

I went right to Miss Annie and told her what Maxine had said. She called her friend who worked for the city. This time she didn't ask me to wait outside.

"Sam, it's Annie," she said. "Is there anything more on Maxine Flooter?"

She listened. After a while she sighed. "I know you shouldn't be," she said. "Just read me the last part."

A minute later she hung up the phone. "The bottom line's the same," she told me, looking thoughtful.

"What do you mean?"

"No one's filed a complaint, though there have been meetings. Without a complaint there can't be a hearing."

"She said she had it all worked out."

"I wonder what she meant by that," Miss Annie said.

"I don't know." I wanted to feel relieved, but somehow I couldn't.

Then Maxine got drunk to beat the band: staggering, weaving, screaming drunk. Bobby came and got me when he saw her. Jerry must have told him about the investigation, so he knew it was important.

"Come quick!" he said. "She's in front of Old Man Meyers' house, raising hell."

We ran down there. She'd gathered a crowd and was entertaining them by breaking beer bottles on the sidewalk. Ronald was nowhere to be seen.

"I'm going to do it!" she screamed, waving a bottle over her head. "You better move back, 'cause I'm going to let it fly."

Mrs. Meyers was holding on to Mister so he wouldn't get too close. He was so mad, his face was purple. "I called the cops!" he yelled. "I'm going to press charges! I've had enough of you, Maxine!"

"You ain't had enough, either!" Maxine threw the bottle. It smashed a few feet in front of them.

"Stop it, now!" Ralph Murphy came out of the crowd, and I came behind him. But Maxine turned fast as a cat. "I'll get you, too!" she screamed. She had another bottle in her hand. "I'm the atomic bomb!" she shouted. "Every single one of you is going to die!"

Bobby slipped behind Maxine and pulled her arms behind her back. The bottle fell to the sidewalk and rolled away. She cussed like he was killing her. "Get off of me! Get off!" She called him every name in the book.

The cops didn't hold her. I talked to Old Man Meyers and his wife and promised to clean up the mess if they'd give her one more chance. They weren't happy about it, but I kept on talking, and finally they agreed just to get rid of me.

The cops drove Maxine home. I didn't follow them; I

didn't want to know if Miss Marlow or anybody else was sitting on her front porch waiting to get in. But I was worried about Ronald. I went down an hour later and banged on the door, but nobody came.

"Etta left a pot of soup on the porch, and it's gone, so I suppose he's had his supper," Miss Annie said. "I'll go around tomorrow morning and leave some sandwiches."

"But who's going to put his pajamas on him?"

"He'll have to sleep in his clothes tonight, I guess." She sighed. "Worse things have happened."

"Maxine said she was going to kill us—she thought the bottle she was holding was a bomb." I sat for a moment. "Miss Annie? She wouldn't hurt Ronald, would she?"

She sighed again. "I don't think so, Vernon. She never has before."

"I'm going back tomorrow. If she won't open the door, I'll go in the window. I want to be sure he's all right."

26

BUT THE NEXT DAY there was no one home. When I turned the knob, the door swung open. The house smelled like booze and garbage and dog mess. Clothes were scattered everywhere. For a minute I didn't notice Brownie cringing in the corner. I called to him and he slunk over as if he expected to be slapped. I could see his ribs. "I'll find some dog food," I muttered.

I looked in the cupboard, but there was nothing but a couple cans of soup and a half-filled jar of macaroni. The sink was piled with dirty dishes. On the table was an empty bottle of whiskey, and next to it Ronald's Converse. I picked them up and held them for a minute. They still looked new. Brownie whimpered. "I'll try the back porch," I told him.

The bag of dog food was sitting there behind the

door. The top was neatly folded, as if someone had taken care that it stay dry. "You haven't been fed for a long time," I said. I stroked his head as he ate.

I let him out when I left, so he'd have the garbage to browse through. And I wrote Maxine a note.

The door was unlocked, so I came in.
I gave Brownie some dog food.
Vernon

That Sunday Maxine and Ronald came to church. I didn't see them at first, because I was sitting in the back with Jerry and Bobby. Then Bobby put his elbow in my ribs. "Look who's here."

I thought he meant a girl. "Who?"

He gestured toward the center aisle, down low.

She was dressed for the occasion: her dress was lime green and the hat she wore looked like a squashed tomato with a veil stuck to it. She had a gold shoe on her right foot, a bedroom slipper on her left, and an orange plastic pocketbook over her arm.

"Here comes Ronald." She'd left him in the aisle ten feet behind her. He had his new clothes on, but he didn't have any socks. He was rocking back and forth. She stopped and yelled for him to hurry up.

"Oh, boy," muttered Jerry. "This is going to be good."

"I'd better try to get them out of here."

"Looks like Father Tom beat you to it."

Father Tom was short for Tomachefski, and if anybody had a shot at calming Maxine down, it was him. He was a big, red-faced guy who spent half his time on the front porch of the rectory drinking beer and listening to the ball game. He was so easygoing that the line outside his confessional on Fridays was always twice as long as the others. Sure enough, he talked to her for a minute, then put his arm around her shoulder. But instead of taking her and Ronald outside, he led them to a pew near the front. I groaned inside. I knew she'd never make it through the mass without opening her mouth.

Father Finn was the celebrant. Maxine started in on him after the hymn. "Hey, baldybean," she yelled. "I've got something to tell you!"

Father Finn froze.

"This is my son Ronald!" She turned toward the congregation. "You all know us, don't you?"

The place was so still, you could have heard a whisper. Out of the corner of my eye I saw one of the ushers in the back stand up.

"I been taking care of Ronald since he was born. Sometimes I did a good job and sometimes I didn't, but he loves me anyway. He wrote down on a piece of paper he's going to give me the national mother-of-the-year award."

Somebody tittered. Father Finn made a sign to the ushers behind Maxine's back. She spun around and shook her fist.

"You're in the same bed with Social Services!" she

screamed. "But you're not going to get Ronald, neither one of you!"

"You are disrupting our worship service," Father Finn said into the microphone. "You must leave immediately."

"Not yet!" Maxine turned back toward us. "I decide what's right for Ronald!" she shouted triumphantly. "And I've decided: Ronald needs family!"

"Family?" Jerry looked at me. I shrugged. But Maxine wasn't done.

"No matter what you think of me, I love Ronald every day!" she yelled. "I love him more than Mary loved Jesus. You all can sit here and pray, but I don't have to pray, because God knows I love Ronald!"

The organ started then, but nobody sang—we were all watching up front. We thought she'd fight the ushers, but instead she grabbed Ronald and pulled him up. They walked up the center aisle with one usher on each side. Ronald was trembling, but Maxine couldn't shut up. Every time she saw someone she knew, she stopped.

"You sure have gotten fat, Bob Bond!

"I saw Ted up at the bar last night, Brenda. He was holding hands with a blond girl.

"Florence, your cat pissed in my yard."

The usher tugged at her elbow. "Get your hands off me!" Maxine hollered. She staggered, and for a moment I thought she might fall. But she pulled herself up on someone's coat. You could smell her breath a mile away.

"I ain't drunk," she muttered to Jean Snyder, who works up at Central Bank. "Least I ain't robbed nobody, like you all do."

Jean only smiled. "Go on, Maxine," she said. "Let us finish the mass."

"I'm going." She was quiet as she came closer. The organist had given up. I could see Ronald's eyes as he flicked them back and forth, back and forth. I ducked low in my seat, but she saw me anyway.

"There's Vernon Dibbs," she told the world. "He don't have the brains God gave a stump."

I guess the guys could tell I was hurting. After church Jerry got his folks to let him stay while they went to visit his brother. We hooked up with Chris, and he set up a game of pickup ball. We came down the block with our bats and gloves. Frank Gilberti was working on his windowboxes.

"You boys going to play baseball?"

"Maybe."

"Play hard—one day you'll make the Orioles."

"Right, Mr. Frank."

We went on. Bobby shook his head. "We're still little kids to him."

I tried to remember the last time I felt like a little kid. I remembered how I used to believe in Santa Claus. I'd draw pictures of the toys I wanted and stick them in the mail slot. No matter what I asked for, there was a pile of presents under the tree Christmas morning, and there was always something special for me. I used to dream about the moment Santa labeled those presents—"for Vernon"—and how he cared about me. When Tony told me the truth, I cried all night.

27

I DIDN'T FORGIVE MAXINE. If I saw her in the street, I turned my back and looked away till she was gone. She'd shout at me, and once it sounded like she was trying to apologize. But I wasn't interested. I just wanted her to leave me alone.

I saw Ronald every chance I got. If Maxine was on the street by herself, I knew he'd be home, and I'd hightail it down there. I'd take a couple sandwiches or a pack of cupcakes, whatever we had in the house. He'd wolf them down and we'd sit and talk. The truth is, I'd talk and Ronald would listen, but by now I knew his face so well it was almost like he *could* talk. He had a thousand expressions, and his arms and legs moved or relaxed according to how he felt. He was always glad to see me, and I felt the same. There was something steady about him, once he was used to you. Just being with him could calm you down.

School let out for Ronald, and then for me. I passed everything but French. My final grade in English was a B–. I showed it to Miss Annie, and she smiled like she'd swallowed a cat.

"I knew you could do it, Vernon! All you needed was a little help."

"A little help! I must've spent a hundred hours studying that damn junk!"

"Vernon, don't curse. Cursing is uncouth."

"Un-what?"

"Uncouth. That means ungentlemanly."

I tried to hold back, but I couldn't. Miss Annie didn't think it was funny. "Every boy should strive to be a gentleman," she said.

"I striven, but I didn't make it."

"Then you must keep trying. You have a strong mind and a strong will—look how you succeeded with your tutoring."

I tried to keep a straight face. "Yes, ma'am."

"Huckleberry Finn was uncouth, but he gained the stature of a gentleman by his concern for his fellow man. You'll read that book one day, Vernon. It's one of the hallmarks of American literature."

"Maybe. The other one you gave me was better than I thought. Sandra read part of it out loud to Ben, and the other day I even read some to Ronald. I showed him the pictures, too. There's a dog in it that looks like Brownie."

Miss Annie nodded. "Ribsy."

"Ronald and I pretended we were dogs. We were barking and howling. Then I saw Maxine on the sidewalk, so I ran out the back door."

"She seemed a little better yesterday. She asked about the garden, and I told her we'd pick some things for them today."

"I don't want to see her, Miss Annie."

"You won't have to. If you help me in the garden, I'll take the vegetables over to their house afterward."

I helped Miss Annie down her steps and across the yard. To my surprise, the rectangle of dirt had sprouted patches of green. But it didn't look like gardens in pictures: the rows weren't straight, and there were sections where hardly anything had come up. Miss Annie didn't seem to mind. She rested her forearms on the chrome bar of the walker. "Those are marigold seedlings—I remember how they looked on the packet." She pointed. "And those with the red stems are baby beets."

"This looks like lettuce."

"It is. Pick a good handful, and pull up five or six of those radishes." She showed me where, and I got down on my knees and did it.

"What's this over here?"

"*Ipomoea*—that's the Latin name for morning glory. They came up on their own. And those dark-green ones aren't what I ordered either."

"I'll pull them up."

"No, let's see how they turn out. It'll make the garden more interesting to have some mystery plants."

"But if they're weeds . . ."

She shook her head. "Weeds flower too, you know. And they can be beautiful."

"Weeds?"

She nodded. I could tell from her spaced-out smile that it was hopeless to argue. She put the stuff I'd picked into a plastic bag. "I'll take it over to them now."

"Remind Maxine about the Special Olympics, okay?"

"That's next Saturday, isn't it?"

I nodded.

"I'll remind her."

"Thanks." I brushed the dirt off my knees and went on up the street.

28

"MAXINE'S LOOKING FOR YOU, VERN," Ben said at suppertime a few days later. "She has something important to tell you."

"I don't care what she has to say."

"It's about Ronald."

"I know about that. Miss Annie said I'm supposed to pick him up at nine Saturday morning."

"You better go early," Steph said. "The way Maxine's been lately, you may have to dress him."

"You're right. We have to catch the nine-thirty bus."

"Maybe I could give you two a ride." Daddy leaned over and switched off the TV. He started stacking the dirty plates.

"Sure—if you want to."

"Just let me know when."

"I'll wash those, Daddy," Steph said. "You've been working all day."

"I'm not going to wash them, but neither are you." He grinned. Everybody looked around. We could tell from his tone of voice something was up.

He held up a beat-up piece of paper. "I made a schedule," he said. "The days of the week are on top, and your names are underneath. There are six of us, so we'll rotate Sundays."

"Let me see that!" We all started grabbing. He'd misspelled a couple things, but you could tell what it meant.

"I can't do Tuesdays," Tony said. "I got science club that night."

"You can trade it off."

"I don't like to wash dishes," Ben said. "I'm too little, anyway."

"I don't mind during the summer, but I got too much homework during the school year," I said. "I can't let my grades slide like I did last fall."

"You'll figure out a way to do it," Daddy said. "You'll have to, all of you."

"It's not fair," Sandra said. "I'm Monday. That's tonight!"

But Daddy didn't bother to answer.

I saw Maxine on the sidewalk outside Milt's. I could tell by the way she was walking she was drunk as sin. "Vernon," she hollered. "I got to tell you something."

"I don't want to hear it."

"You better hear it. If you don't—"

"I'm too stupid to understand, okay, Maxine?" I screamed like she was two blocks away instead of fifteen feet. She drew back. Her face twisted from sadness to rage.

"You'll be sorry!" she yelled.

"Right." I turned and walked away.

She was out for the whole afternoon. I went down and sat with Ronald awhile. We watched a little TV, and I showed him the sports section of the paper. It had lots of photographs of baseball stars, and I told him who they were. But he seemed restless. "Want to go for a walk?" I asked. He nodded.

We went up to my block. We looked for Bobby and Chris, but they were off someplace, so we ended up buying a couple packs of chips and sitting on the steps in the sun. There were fluffy white clouds rolling across the sky like trucks. I showed them to Ronald, and he sat with his neck craned for a long time, looking.

Rat-a-tat! Rat-a-tat! Ben and Mitchell came out of the alley, carrying make-believe guns. They stopped when they saw us. "We got chalk," Ben said. "Miss Etta gave it to us." He reached in his pocket and showed me a couple hunks of colored chalk.

"What are you going to do with it?"

"Go up to Mr. Ward's and write cuss words on his sidewalk."

I used to do that when I was little. Still, I couldn't stop myself from bugging them.

"What would your old lady say if she saw you, Mitchell? I bet she'd tan your hide."

Mitchell put his hands on his hips. His skinny little butt stuck out behind him. "My mom don't come home till six! She ain't going to see nothing!"

"I know you'd get a whipping," I told Ben.

"You won't say nothing." Ben was defiant. But instead of getting mad, I laughed. Something about those little runts tickled me. "They think they're big," I told Ronald. "Look at them, seven years old, and they think they know it all."

"We do!" They started showing off for real now, doing flips and cartwheels. They pretended to disco, and Mitchell sang his own goofy version of "The Star-Spangled Banner." Ben tried to walk on his hands. A piece of chalk tumbled out of his pocket and rolled in front of us. Ronald bent over and picked it up quick.

"He wants to draw a picture! Let him draw, Vern!" The boys were hopping up and down. Ronald shrank back toward me.

"You guys are scaring him."

"Show him how to draw."

"I'm no good at drawing."

"Here!" Ben grabbed the chalk and drew a stick dog. "See, Ronald—it's like Brownie."

Ronald looked at me. I took the chalk and guided his

hand: "There you go."

"He wants to do another one—help him, Vern."

I helped him again. He was breathing hard.

"You made a dog, Ronald." Ben looked him in the face. Ronald's foot was twitching. He let go of the chalk, and it rolled away, down the sidewalk. Ben ran and got it. "Make another one with him, Vern."

"No, that's enough. He's getting all shook up."

"That's 'cause he wants to draw another one. Don't you, Ronald?"

Ronald nodded, but I shook my head. "That's enough, Ben. We have to clean this up as it is."

"But he wants to!"

"You don't know what he wants."

"I do too. He wants to draw, don't you Ronald?"

Ronald nodded. I took the chalk out of Ben's hand and stuck it in my pocket. Ronald stamped his foot and pointed to the sidewalk.

"No," I said.

He glared at me.

"No."

He pointed to the picture.

"No."

He opened his mouth like he was going to start screaming. But instead of a scream, a word dropped out so suddenly that all of us, even Ronald, just stood there staring. "Daw," he said. "Daw." The second one was so quiet it was almost a whisper.

"He said dog." Ben whispered, too.

"Stop!" I was sweating. "We might not have heard right."

But there was no stopping Ronald. "Daw!" he said.

"He can talk! Ronald can talk! Hey, everybody, come out! We taught Ronald how to talk!" Ben and Mitchell were shrieking. A few neighbors poked their heads out to see what the fuss was about.

"It's nothing!" I said. "Ben and Mitchell, stop!"

"He said dog, Mrs. Murphy! It was clear as a bell!"

"Are you sure, Benjamin?"

"Yes, ma'am!"

Ronald was grinning. "Daw!" he said happily. He pointed at the sidewalk till I led him away.

I don't know why it scared me but it did. I thought I knew Ronald, you know? But it turned out he was changing, just like everything else.

I had to tell Maxine. I went down to the house that evening. She was lying on the couch. Ronald was on a kitchen chair, watching TV.

"Maxine?"

"Uhhhh . . ." Her eyes opened enough to see who it was. I could smell the booze on her breath.

"Something happened today. I took Ronald up the block, and we drew pictures on the sidewalk. I took the chalk away, and he tried to say dog. He must have tried five or six times."

Maxine groaned. She raised herself up on one elbow. "Get out," she said.

"He might be able to talk, if somebody works with him."

"Get out, Vernon." Her voice was thick. She sank back on the couch and closed her eyes.

I made Ronald some soup, the kind where you pour the mix in a cup and add hot water. There was a box of crackers on the same shelf. It wasn't much, but it was better than nothing.

He didn't say dog or anything while I was there. The TV was playing, but he wasn't paying attention. His eyes looked closed, even though they weren't. I figured he was tired.

29

By THE TIME I GOT TO Miss Annie, she'd heard the story from Ben and Mitchell. She didn't believe it right off. I had to go through it bit by bit.

"Fascinating," she said when I was done. "Somebody should tell Ronald's teacher."

"I'm not telling her anything. She's the one who caused all this upset in the first place."

Miss Annie looked surprised. "Do you really believe that?"

It was my turn to hesitate. "Before she got involved, Maxine and Ronald were doing okay."

"That's not true. Maxine was in jail before Christmas."

"But you and Mrs. Moore took care of Ronald till she got out."

"Others helped, too. But he was lonely."

"He would have been more lonely somewhere else. At least he knew you and me and everybody else on the block."

She sighed. "That's true."

"Everybody needs a home, right? And this is Ronald's home—this whole neighborhood. He knows places in Tenley Heights even I never noticed." I told her about the yard with all the statues, and the bitchy woman. She smiled.

"Eleanor Pappas. She's not as bad as you make her out to be, Vernon."

"How do *you* know her?"

"I've lived here longer than you have, remember? And after I retired, I took a walk every day. There are a lot of houses and faces that I learned by heart."

"Did you know me?"

"Yes, and your brothers and sisters, too. Of course I didn't really *know* you—but I knew who you were, and where you lived, and who your parents were. I knew you and Robert Sullivan and Jerome Roland and Christopher Murphy liked to get together on the corner of Pine and Independence streets. In fact, I think we may have exchanged greetings there."

"Uhhhh . . . yeah." I could feel my face turn red. "Like you said, I didn't really *know* you then."

She nodded. "It takes an effort to become friends with somebody different."

"Like Ronald."

"Like Ronald, or Maxine, or Eleanor Pappas."

"I'll never be friends with her. She's gross."

"She's actually quite interesting. Can you believe she speaks five languages? Her father was Greek and her mother German, so she learned those and English as she grew up. She studied French in high school and college, and she married a merchant seaman who spoke very little English—he was a Saudi, you see. So she learned Arabic as well."

"Miss Annie—"

"Oh!" She looked startled. "Yes, Vernon?"

"What about Ronald? About his talking, I mean."

"We need to tell his teachers. They have the training to help him develop. Who knows what Ronald could be saying a year from now?"

"You don't understand! Miss Marlow's trying to take Ronald away!"

"I *do* understand. But I also know it's not fair to let him be less than he can be."

"Even if he ends up someplace else?"

"There's no reason to think he will. After all, he didn't speak his first word at school. He did it here, in Tenley Heights, with you."

"That's true." I knew I should feel better, but I couldn't. I kept thinking of Ronald's eyes last night, when Maxine was drunk on the couch. Seeing those eyes, you wouldn't have believed he was the person who'd been outside with Ben and Mitchell and me that same afternoon.

———

That night I couldn't sleep. After a while I went downstairs to check out the refrigerator. The lights were out, but I heard the radio, like before, and Daddy was at the kitchen table. This time he didn't seem as surprised to see me.

"We meet again," he said. "Have a seat, Vern."

"How come you're up?" I asked.

"I like to hear a few oldies before I go to bed."

"A few! It's almost one o'clock."

He shrugged. "They help me think."

"About what?"

"Everything."

I poured myself a glass of milk and drank it down. "Do you figure things out, sitting here?"

"No. But sometimes I'll get an idea or two, after I sort through the questions. Other times they'll come to me in the morning while I'm shaving."

"Is that when you thought of the clean-up schedule?"

He nodded.

"I didn't like that one."

"Nobody did, except Steph. She liked it a lot."

I steadied my head between my hands. "Everything's changing. How can you figure out what to do when things are different every day?"

"Are you thinking about Ronald?"

"Yeah, that's one thing, the biggest, I guess."

"What's to figure out?"

"Miss Annie says we should tell the teachers at his school about his trying to talk. She says they're trained to help him, and we're not."

Daddy nodded.

"But Miss Marlow's been checking up on Maxine. She knows she's a drunk. She may have met with Social Services about putting Ronald in foster care."

"You think talking to her would make that worse?" He sounded calm, like there was no reason to be scared. That reminded me of Miss Annie. But they hadn't been inside Maxine's house when it reeked of whiskey and garbage. They hadn't seen Miss Marlow's face when she'd asked about special activities for Ronald. Even back then, with the house and Maxine at their best, she'd seemed to feel Ronald needed more. Who knows how many times she'd visited since then? As far as what she'd seen, I was afraid to think about it. Her face, Maxine's, Ronald's, flashed at me like a movie I couldn't turn off. Daddy just sat there, watching me. "What do you think?" he asked again.

I was like a soda bottle that was shook up once too often. "I don't KNOW!"

"Shhhh! You'll wake the others."

"I can't be quiet! I don't know what to do!"

Daddy sat there with his mouth open.

I didn't mean to say the next part, but I did. "Mom would know! She'd tell me!"

Daddy grabbed me across the table. "She's not here!"

"Let go!"

"Not yet." He pulled me up so we were face to face. For the first time I realized I was looking down at him.

158

"We have to help each other," he said.

"Nobody can help me."

"I can try."

"No, you can't. You can't even read and write."

If I'd hurt him, it didn't show. "I'm going to learn."

I closed my eyes, but the tears edged out anyway. "Why did she do it?"

"Miss Marlow?"

"Not her—Mom!"

"Oh, Vernon!" He put his face right up close. I could smell his sweat, his hair, even the soap powder he washed his shirts in. He'd smelled the same ever since I was a little kid.

I grabbed him and held on for all I was worth.

"If she'd been real important, they would have saved her," I said later. "I've seen on TV where they save people who are halfway torn apart. They spend millions of dollars on them."

"But there's no guarantee how they'll come out of it, Vern. Think about Etta's father—he can't move, he can't hardly talk."

"I'd want her here even if she couldn't talk. I'd take care of her."

"If it had happened that way, we all would." He sighed. "She worked too hard—I know that now. If I could change it, I'd go back and stop her. But that chance is gone." He looked right at me. "As for being kept alive by machines, Mary wouldn't have wanted that."

159

"But what about us? What about what we want?"

"We have to help each other get what we want. But no one person is home free. Steph can't be stuck with the cooking and the dishes every night. And Tony has to think about all of us, not just himself and his career."

"And me?"

"I want you to teach me to read."

"Are you kidding?"

He didn't crack a smile. "No. I'm pretty sure you'd be the best one. You're patient, and you know what it's like not to catch on to something right away."

I stared at him. "Why didn't you learn in school?"

"I was always scared the teacher would call on me and I wouldn't know the answer. I got so I wouldn't even open the book because it made me feel bad. Then I found out I could get a job without being able to read. We needed the money, so I did. I felt good about it for a few years. Then I went through a period when I had to fake it, which was awful. Right near the end of that I met Mary, and she saved me. She read for me."

"She could have taught you."

"We were so busy, we never made the time. There was always a baby crawling up my leg just when I got a moment to spare. And she had her hands in the bread dough, or in the sink—you know how it was."

"Yeah, I remember." I did, too. I'd be sitting on the kitchen floor trying to color and either Ben or Sandra would come slithering over and grab the page. I'd start to yell. Mom would pick me and my stuff up and put us

160

at the kitchen table. I smiled.

"What are you thinking about?" Daddy asked.

"The way it used to be."

"I like to think about that, too. When I sit here listening to the radio, I remember those times. For a while I felt more alive then, remembering, than I did in real life. But that's changing. You kids can't grow up without me. You and Tony need help getting along, and Steph's dating—think about that! Last time I looked over my shoulder, she was Sandra's age."

"I don't see what she likes about Jimmy."

Daddy smiled. "Maybe it's the red hair."

"He could go bald. Then she'd be stuck with him."

"I don't think she's thinking that far ahead. I hope not."

We sat there a little longer. The clock on the stove said two thirty. "I better go to bed," Daddy murmured. "I've got work tomorrow."

"But you haven't told me what to do about Ronald."

He shook his head slowly. "Vern, I don't know what to do."

"You mean I have to figure it out for myself."

"What I mean is it may not make a difference what you figure out."

"It does!"

He didn't answer, but his fingers brushed my back as I got up. I didn't say good night; I was so tired I don't even remember climbing the steps and lying down. Maybe I did it in my sleep.

30

I SAW MAXINE ONCE MORE before the Special Olympics. I was standing by myself on the corner when she came by. She was dressed shabbily, in a worn coat and built-up shoes, the kind old ladies wear. Her eyes were on the sidewalk, so she didn't see me. I don't know why, but I spoke to her. It took her a moment to realize it was me.

"Vernon?"

"Yeah."

She stood there with her arms at her sides. Her eyes looked dull.

"Everything's happened, hasn't it?"

"What do you mean?"

"Between us."

"I don't know."

"I'll see you sometime."

"Tomorrow—remember? I'm taking Ronald to the Olympics."

"Mrs. Moore's getting him ready. He'll wear those shoes."

She walked on like she was in a fog. I watched to see if she was headed for Milt's, but she turned left and kept walking. After a while her coat disappeared among the dark walls of the rowhouses.

The Special Olympics changed everything, not just for Ronald but for me.

Daddy dropped Ronald and me at the main gate. Ronald looked good. Mrs. Moore had ironed his pants, and of course he had on his Converse. She'd even sent a baseball cap with him, in case the sun was bright.

The woman at the registration table gave us name tags and coupons good for all the hot dogs and soda we wanted. I asked her what events Ronald should enter. She smiled. "What does he like to do?"

I had to think for a second. "He likes to watch TV, and to eat, and to take walks. And he likes dogs."

"How about a big lunch, and then some of the walking races? You can walk beside him if you need to."

"Okay."

"Here's a map of the area. The food concessions are marked in red."

We went right over and got ourselves two jumbo Cokes and two hot dogs. While we were eating, Ronald twisted around in his chair and waved.

163

"Hi, Ronald."

A retarded girl stepped out of the stream of people on the sidewalk. She was chubby and wore glasses with red frames. Ronald grinned.

"This is Lily." The tall man behind her must have been her dad. He had on a business suit. "These two are in class together," he said.

"Miss Marlow's?"

"Yeah!" Lily nodded. "Hi, Ronald!"

Ronald stuck out one foot.

"Red ones!" Lily said.

"With white checks. They're eyecatchers." Her dad winked at me.

"My friends and I helped Ronald pick them out."

"Are you Ronald's brother?"

"No, just a friend from the neighborhood."

"We'll see you later, friend." He shook my hand, and Lily did too. I was surprised he did that. He was the kind of person you'd see downtown, or in the business section of the newspaper. I slurped down the last of my soda. "Jerry's here somewhere, and his brother John. Let's see if we can find them."

We didn't find them right away. There were zillions of people around, and lots of them caught your eye and held it. They had bodies and faces that didn't fit quite right, and some of them had the same expression Ronald did when I first saw him: scared. Maybe they thought you were going to stare, or that you wouldn't like them because of the way they looked or the way they were. Once you smiled, that usually changed.

"Vernon, this is Adrian."

The soft voice sent a chill through me, but when I turned to face her, her eyes were as warm as they'd been that first time, months ago. She was wearing white shorts and a pink top that ended just above her hips. A scrawny little girl was clutching her hand.

"Miss Marlow!"

"I've been looking for you and Ronald."

"You have?"

She nodded. "I wanted to make sure someone had shown you around and given you food coupons for your lunch. And I want to offer you two a ride home. I live in Medfield, so I drive right by Tenley Heights on the way to my apartment."

"I've seen you a few times. You drive a red Honda, don't you?"

She nodded. "The backseat's a mess, but we'll clean it up enough to make room for you." She leaned over and took Ronald's hand, just for a minute. He smiled.

"I hope you have a wonderful time. I'll meet you at the gate at five o'clock."

I wanted to hate her, but I couldn't. The little girl was clinging to her hand like she'd die if she let go. Miss Marlow didn't seem to mind. "Adrian's mother couldn't make it," she explained. "I have to find her a coach for the hundred-yard dash."

"Maybe I could do it. Ronald's races aren't till after one."

"That would be wonderful. All you'd have to do is run beside her and show her the checkpoints. The race is in ten minutes, over at the quad." She showed me where it was. "Thanks, Vernon," she said. Her voice was soft as melted butter.

Adrian didn't win her race, but she sure enjoyed trying. I kept a few feet ahead of her so she'd push herself, and she did. When we got to the tape we were neck and neck. Afterward she threw her arms around me.

Later we hooked up with Jerry's family. His brother John was a nice kid. He was a couple years older than Jerry, but you couldn't tell that by looking at him—he was shorter than Jerry, and heavier. He had the green eyes that run in the family, and he was pretty good at sports, like the rest of them. He placed high in all the events he entered. They were proud of him.

Ronald didn't place high in anything, but he had a great day. Whatever he tried, the crowds cheered him on. A lot of them knew him from school. He had more friends than I'd ever imagined.

He got five green ribbons for participating. We pinned them on his shirt. He ate six hot dogs, and the pop he drank must have set a record. He pointed a couple times when we saw dogs, and once he looked at me shyly and moved his lips: "Daaw."

I'd made up my mind to tell her in the car. But she started talking when we first got in and kept it up, telling me about Adrian: how shy she'd been when she started school, and how much she'd progressed. "She's really come out of her shell," she said, turning the corner onto the highway.

"I liked her."

"You have a knack for working with special children, Vernon."

"I didn't at first—well, with Ronald I didn't really know him, so he made me nervous. But then we became friends. After that, I kept learning more and more about him—he's complicated, you know?"

"Yes, he feels deeply. It must be frustrating to have strong emotions and not be able to express them."

"There's something you should know about that." I swallowed. "Ronald tried to say dog last week. He tried four or five times. And he tried again today. It comes out 'daaw.'" I glanced at the backseat to see if Ronald was listening, but he'd fallen asleep.

Miss Marlow turned toward me. "That's *wonderful*! I'll make a note of that when I prepare his records."

"I wasn't sure whether to tell you."

She nodded as if she understood. "It's been hard, hasn't it? There were so many aspects of his home life that were good—like you, Vernon. In fact all the neighbors seemed to care about Ronald."

"They *do* care. Mrs. Moore got him ready today. She even ironed his pants."

"You'll miss him, won't you?"

I thought I'd heard her wrong. "What?"

"I said you'll miss him." Then she saw my face. "Oh, Vernon, I'm sorry. Miss Flooter said she'd tell you."

"Tell me what?"

"Ronald's leaving next week. He's going to live with his aunt and uncle in North Carolina."

I didn't believe her, not at first.

She sighed. "His mom's gone back and forth on the decision. She didn't make up her mind for sure until two weeks ago. But she wanted him to be with family."

"Family! They're not family! Ronald doesn't even know them!"

"That's true."

"Maxine just told you that to get you off her case! She's not sending Ronald anywhere!"

"I saw her sign the papers, Vernon."

"Why?"

"You know why."

"I don't," I lied. "I don't know why."

"You wrote me after the fair. But I knew about Ronald's problems before then. The police had recommended him for foster care a year ago, but it didn't go through." She stopped. "I can see you're upset, and I understand."

"I wrote to you. You should have called me."

"I wanted to, but these things are confidential. I asked Miss Flooter to tell you, and she said she would."

I remembered Ben's message that night at supper: "She says it's important." Sweat beaded on my forehead. "She can change her mind," I said.

"She's signed the custody declaration."

"That doesn't mean it's final."

"It is." Her voice was firm, and she kept her eyes on the highway.

"You can drop me off right here," I said.

"Vernon . . ."

"Let me out!"

She pulled over, and I got out and slammed the door. I didn't look at her. The thought of her blond hair and gentle voice made me feel like throwing up.

She'd dropped Ronald off by the time I got to Maxine's. There were kids playing catch in the street, but I ignored their shouting and pounded on the peeling doorframe. She came right away. She was dressed in a ratty bathrobe. "I tried to tell you," she said weakly. The sweet, sharp smell of liquor washed over me.

"Why?"

"I'll know where he is, and who he's with."

"You never mentioned him having an aunt and uncle. I don't believe it."

"There's a lot I never mentioned, but it's true."

"You're giving him away."

"They'd take him otherwise." Her voice was fast and low.

"If you loved him, you wouldn't do this." I spit the words at her. She started to cry.

"Ronald's all I have."

"You could have quit drinking! You could have pulled yourself together!"

"I tried." The tears rolled down her flabby cheeks.

"This is his home! This is where he lives!" I waved my arm at the block behind me. Kids gathered on the sidewalk to hear the argument. "You can't send him away!" I yelled.

Something moved behind Maxine. Ronald's head appeared over her shoulder. He grabbed her arm.

"You can't do it," I repeated.

"It's done," she said simply, and she closed the door.

31

MISS ANNIE HAD FOUND OUT that morning. I guess Maxine came over after Ronald left and spilled her guts about what she'd done.

"I didn't believe her right away," Miss Annie said. "But she showed me a copy of the paper she'd signed. It had a notary stamp and the court's seal on it."

"She should go back and say she changed her mind."

"She won't. She feels she's done what's best." Miss Annie took a white tablet out of the little pill case she kept on the table by the sofa. She swallowed the pill with a sip of water. "Did you hear where Ronald's going?" she asked slowly.

"I don't want to hear!"

"Her sister and brother-in-law live on a small farm in the foothills of North Carolina. They have all kinds of animals and a big garden. There's a state university with a special education school just twelve miles away. It's one of the best schools in the country."

"North Carolina is a hick state. There's nothing down there but dust and tobacco!"

Miss Annie continued as if I hadn't said anything. "They've been married for thirty years, and they've raised five children of their own. They wrote Maxine and said they'd be glad to have Ronald for however long she wanted. They said they'd treat him like one of their own."

"They don't even know him!"

She nodded, but she didn't look right at me like she usually did. "That's true. But they'll get to know him. It will take time."

I stared at her. "You're going along with it."

This time she did look at me. "I think he'll be better off."

"How can you say that?"

"He needs to grow, just like the rest of us. He's tried, and you've been a big help. But if he had a real home, with people to talk to him and care for him every day, he wouldn't have to spend his energy wondering when he'll get his next meal. He'd be able to put down roots."

"He's not a plant!"

"He needs food and sunshine and loving care."

"*This* is his home!"

We stared at each other. "We disagree," Miss Annie said softly.

I didn't say anything. Behind the sofa, on her carved desk, books were stacked like a rickety tower. I wanted to knock them down, to rip out the pages and throw them all over the room.

32

HE LEFT ON A TUESDAY. By then everyone in Tenley Heights knew he was going. Some, like Jerry and his folks, thought it was a good thing. Others shook their heads. "She'll take the bus down and yank him back up here before the leaves drop," Etta said.

"That court paper won't let her, hon. She's given him up for good."

"Not if I know Maxine." Etta looked down the row of porches like she might see her coming any minute. "As mean as she is, she loves that boy. She won't be able to live without him."

Bobby stood by me. "What the hell's Ronald going to do way down in the country?" he said. "Is he supposed to wear his Converse to slop the hogs?"

"Beats me."

"It don't make no sense, man. No sense at all."

At home I hardly talked about it. Everybody knew how bad I felt. They went out of their way to be nice. Ben and Sandra gave me an Orioles cap for Ronald.

"We found it in the stadium parking lot," Ben explained. "I was going to keep it for myself, but it's too big."

"It should fit him real good."

"Mrs. Moore's knitting him a sweater. She's got the back and one sleeve done already."

"I'm giving him a picture of me," Ben said. "I wrote my name on it."

"He can't read, dummy!"

"Maybe he'll learn. Miss Annie says there's no telling what he'll learn down there."

I tried to see him. Every time I went down, the door was locked. I could hear the TV playing, and if I knocked loud enough Brownie would yap. Once or twice I heard Maxine hollering to go away. She didn't even know who was out there.

Mitchell caught me on Monday. His little sister Keesha was dragging after him like a puppy on a leash. Every now and then he took off after her, but she always came back.

"Vernon, they're here," he said.

"Who?"

"The relatives. They got an old-model Buick with a

North Carolina license plate."

"They're *from* North Carolina. What do you expect?"

"The lady's on the heavy side—you know." He held his arms out from his sides. "And the man is old and skinny. I asked him was he related to Ronald and he said, 'Yes-siree-bob.'" Mitchell imitated a southern accent. "Then he give me two Milky Ways and a stick of gum." He looked over his shoulder. "That's why Keesha's following me around."

"Why don't you give her some?"

"'Cause I was the one went up to him. Keesha hid in the alley."

"Did Maxine let them in?"

"She must have, because I went back down after a while. The car was still there and they weren't on the porch anymore."

I didn't know what to say. I'd been thinking maybe they wouldn't show, but they had.

I went down again that evening. A gray-haired woman answered the door. Her eyes were clear blue, and her face was smoother than Maxine's. She was wearing a baggy dress.

"Are you a friend of Ronnie's?" She smiled.

"His name is Ronald," I said stiffly. "I was hoping to see him."

"Come on in, honey." She opened the door. "He's just sitting watching TV."

I sat with him awhile. He hardly looked at me, and

the room was so noisy with the two of them talking to Maxine that I couldn't hear myself think. They tried to talk to me, too, but I only answered yes or no. I figured if they were taking Ronald, I didn't have to be nice to them, to boot.

Before I left, I told him I'd come back tomorrow. He looked at me with scared eyes.

"I heard they got all kinds of animals down there," I said. "Dogs and cats and cows and pigs, even a pony."

"We sure do," the woman said. "We got a litter of puppies born three weeks ago. Cutest little things you ever did see."

Ronald's eyes clung to mine.

"I'll come back tomorrow," I promised him.

Half the neighborhood was down there Tuesday morning. A lot of them had presents: fudge and base-ball cards and cookies and dollar bills. I'd brought the hat and a picture of myself sitting on the steps of our house. I cut out a drawing of Ribsy from the Beezus book and stuck it on the back.

Nobody talked to me except to say hi. There was nothing they could say. Frank Gilberti clapped me on the back, and Etta gave me a piece of fudge. Miss Annie was there, crying her eyes out. Even the woman with the junky statues in her yard showed up.

They brought Ronald out at ten o'clock. They stood on either side of him, the two of them. The man was holding a pasteboard box with Ronald's clothes inside.

The woman cleared her throat. "I want to thank you," she said. "There's an awful lot of places that wouldn't have cared for Ronald the way you-all have."

Somebody asked, "Where's Maxine?"

"She said good-bye inside. She's all torn up, poor thing."

The crowd came forward then, giving Ronald whatever they'd brought, until his arms were so full, they had to start laying stuff on top of the clothes. Somebody had a paper bag, and we stuck things in that, too, calling, "Look, Ronald, this is from me. Think of me when you take it down."

He didn't want to get in the car. The old man offered him candy, but Ronald threw it on the ground and stomped his foot. I noticed he was wearing his Converse. He twisted and turned, looking for someone he could trust. Our eyes locked. I shook my head. There was no way I was going to put him in that car. Finally Mrs. Moore took him by the arm and talked to him in her gentle voice. You could see him start to relax. After a while she led him over to the backseat of the Buick, and he did get in. They closed the door fast. He stuck his face up to the window, staring out.

"Good-bye, Ronald!" Everyone was waving. "Take care of yourself! Have a good trip!"

I almost let him go. The Buick backed around until it was facing uphill. Ronald's face was clear in the window. He was looking right at me.

"Good-bye," I whispered. I put my hand on the outside of the glass, and he leaned his face against it. The Buick started to move. I went with it, walking, then trotting alongside. In mid block it picked up speed and I had to lope. My cowboy boots clacked against the pavement. Ronald's face stayed still under my hand.

"Go, Vernon!" The little kids cheered me on, and I heard some older voices, too, Chris and Bobby and Jerry. The car headed into my own block. I saw Steph standing on the sidewalk, with Tony beside her. Daddy's car was parked next to the house. I remember thinking, He's supposed to be at work. Mrs. Murphy called and waved, and so did Etta's brother. I ran past the gang in front of Milt's. "Good-bye," they called. Somebody hollered, "Look at him go!"

I was running full out. The old man gunned the Buick, but I kept up. Maybe they thought I was trying to stop them, and maybe I was. They speeded up. I thought: Steal second! and that helped me pump deeper into what was left. They hit the corner at Pine and York and didn't even slow down. I was with them, with Ronald, but my chest was on fire and I couldn't find more air. The Buick leaped forward. I jumped, too, but my heel hit the curb and snapped. The car went on. I lurched and fell.

I hit the ground rolling and didn't stop until I smashed into a concrete wall, then flipped back onto the grass. I hurt everywhere, but I was still alive: there was a pop bottle under my ribs, and the grass stunk like dog mess. My chest ached so bad I couldn't even cry. I could hear myself gasping like a fish dying on the bank of a pond. My legs were trembling. I heard voices, and someone said sharply, "Stay back!"

I tried to speak, but nothing came out. I hurt all over. A hand moved up my legs and back, feeling for broken bones. It moved around my neck and rested on my face. It smelled familiar.

"Vernon," Daddy said. "I'm here."